NICOLE MACCARRON

Hazel's Shadow

Acknowledgements

A special thank you to Katie Stobbart and Jess Wind for their editing skills and advice. Thank you both for making editing more fun!

Contents

The Shadow

When Hazel was six years old, she woke to find a disembodied shadow standing at the end of her bed. She thought her cat, Salt, had let out a spitting hiss, but she was sleeping over at Gran's new house, and Gran had no cats. As other shadows in the room formed back into furniture, Hazel remembered her twin bed at home was against a wall, and not a queen sandwiched by a dresser and a nightstand. At home, it would have been her teddy bear nightlight giving off a faint glow, not the plug-in scent dispenser; the heavy green curtains would have been floaty and white.

"Gran?" she asked the shadow, hoping she was mistaken and her grandmother would answer.

Her sister, Kelly, stirred beside her.

"Graaan?" she called a little louder, fearing that Gran was, in fact, in the other room.

She kept her eyes fixed on the shadow as she reached over to shake her little sister. It took a menacing step closer and hissed again.

"*Gran!*"

Kelly started awake and began to cry. Hazel whipped the blankets over herself and hunkered down face-to-face with her sister.

"It's okay," she cooed, her voice trembling as she stroked Kelly's arm, "it's okay."

She was used to soothing the four-year-old, and the words were automatic. She felt a presence at her back, like the shadow was looming over her now. The words came faster.

"It's okay, it's okay, it's okay…"

"Hazel?" came Gran's voice at last, and the overhead light flicked on.

Someone pulled the blankets back and Hazel screamed aloud. To her relief, Gran's freckled face appeared. Hazel threw herself into her grandmother's arms.

"It's okay," Gran said, stroking Hazel's tangled, brown hair as she joined her on the edge of the bed.

Hazel peered under her arm. The shadow hadn't fled with the light. It stood in the exact same spot, its limbs stretched and unnatural. Hazel's skin crawled.

"Gran, what is that?" she squeaked, breaking out in sweat.

Gran leaned back to look at Hazel's face. "What is what, love?"

Hazel pointed.

Gran looked, but reached over to touch Kelly's hair at the same time. The little girl's cries were already subsiding as she fell back asleep.

"In the closet, you mean?" Gran asked. "Don't worry, there's no one there. Would you feel better if I checked for you?"

"No, not the closet, the shadow—"

"It's just a shadow, my girl. Watch." Gran turned on the bedside lamp and the remaining shadows fled. "See how all the shadows move and change because of the light?"

"No!" Hazel cried, her voice shrill. "It didn't move! It's right there!"

The shadow was standing, so obvious to Hazel, mere feet from Gran. Hazel could hear her heart in her ears. She could see the hint of a grin.

"Get away from it, Gran!" She tried to pull the old woman onto the bed.

Instead, Gran stood up and walked through the shadow. Hazel gasped. Gran wandered the room, waving her arms to show that there was no one there. But now there was no one between Hazel and the shadow, which returned its gaze to her, unfazed by Gran. Hazel shrunk back and started to cry.

From the other side of the room, Gran sighed. "Why don't I stay with you until you fall back asleep?"

Hazel didn't answer. The old woman passed through the shadow again, and turned off the main light. She lifted the blankets and settled in, fluffing her pillow before pulling Hazel close.

The shadow flashed to the bedside, and Hazel gasped again. Gran continued stroking her hair, trying to calm her. Hazel stared, eye-to-eye with the face menacing over Gran's shoulder, long after Gran's breathing evened out and her hand went still.

* * *

"Who are you talking to?" Kelly, now five, asked as she wandered into the sunlit room Hazel had to herself at home.

"The little girl who used to live next door," Hazel replied. She addressed the girl beside her, "This is my sister."

Hazel was sitting cross-legged on a rug in front of her small doll house. Kelly sat down across from her.

"What does she look like?" Kelly asked.

"She has long curly hair and she's wearing a blue shirt and a pink skirt," Hazel answered.

"What's her name?"

"Jessica."

"Can I play with you?" Kelly asked.

Hazel turned to Jessica. Jessica smiled.

"You can play with us," Hazel said, but couldn't resist adding a rule of her own, "as long as you don't mess up the game."

"Can I have the brown-haired girl?"

"No!" Hazel said, snatching up the doll. "That's Jessica's." She placed it in front of Jessica's knees, smoothing the skirt and hair. "You can have this one."

She handed Kelly her least favourite doll. Kelly started picking out fancy clothes.

"No, Jessica says we're going to the park," Hazel objected, so Kelly dropped a sparkly dress and picked out some shorts.

They crammed the dolls into a toy car and Kelly raced it around the dollhouse.

"That's too fast," Hazel said as the plastic tires made a terrible squeak on the hardwood floor.

"Jessica says we're going to crash!" Kelly cried.

"No, she doesn't!"

Kelly continued to wing the car around before *eeerching* to a stop and tossing a few dolls out. Jessica was close to tears.

"Are you okay?" Kelly's doll asked Hazel's.

"You're wrecking the game!" Hazel cried, getting up to snatch the dolls back.

"No, I'm not!"

Hazel turned back to Jessica for support, but heard only the sound of the girl's shoes on the stairs.

"Look what you did! You made Jessica go away!"

"No, I didn't!"

The arguing grew louder until their mom stepped in. Jolene was a thin nurse, always on her feet at the hospital and as the only parent at home. She ordered the girls into separate rooms.

"Hazel," she said, taking a doll from Hazel's hand as she sulked. "Your sister just wants to play with you. You have to take her ideas sometimes."

"She made Jessica—"

"Who?"

"My friend, Jessica! Kelly made—"

"That's enough," Jolene interrupted. She gave her a pointed look. "Your *friend* needs to take her ideas too."

Hazel glowered at the rug as her mom went to check on Kelly. The injustice of it all faded into piercing sadness as she wondered if Jessica would ever come back. Sometimes they didn't. She dumped the dolls back into the dollhouse, wishing she had someone to talk to, someone alive to believe her.

Ghosts

A fly landed on Hazel's windshield. She groaned, raising her sunglasses to wipe sweat from her eyes. She had to be back at school in fifteen minutes, but traffic was at a standstill. An ambulance had gone wailing past a few minutes earlier, and Hazel suspected there had been an accident. She had just wanted to run to a store during lunch, and now she was going to miss an important class during the last month of high school. Peeling her thick legs apart, she cranked the fan, regretting as usual that her cheap junker didn't have air-conditioning. She pulled strands of her long hair off her neck and tied a ponytail.

When she looked back up, there was someone sitting in the passenger seat. She jumped, shaking the car. The man was looking at her with pleading brown eyes. Hazel stifled a giggle at how high she had jumped. Even after 17 years, ghosts still managed to scare her.

"I don't know what to do," he said, his voice cracking.

He was in shock. Hazel sobered herself up and took in his clothes. Subtle lettering stitched onto his shoulder read 'Leather Canada.'

"You were on a motorcycle?"

He nodded, now staring at the dashboard.

"No helmet?"

His hand brushed his short-cropped hair. Hazel peered out the window while she waited for his answer, trying to catch a glimpse of the accident.

"It must have fallen off," he said.

"Good," she replied, turning back to him. "That you were wearing one."

"Am I dead?" he asked.

"If you stay in my car, yes," Hazel said, blunt from practice, but still compassionate. "Your body doesn't have a fighting chance if you're away for too long. Go. Now. Get back in there."

He was slow to process the message, but nodded and got to his feet as if the car wasn't there anymore. Hazel watched him dawdle through the middle lane of traffic in a daze. She willed him to hurry up. At last he must have spotted his body, because he broke into a run and Hazel lost sight of him. She wished him luck and sighed. Now she had another journal entry to write on top of her homework.

An hour late to her afternoon class, Hazel decided to skip the rest of the day and postpone her teacher's accusations until tomorrow instead. She was surprised when she pulled into her driveway to find Kelly waiting for her. Kelly ran to the driver's side door.

"What are you doing home?" Hazel asked.

"We have to go to the hospital," she replied through the open window, her face stricken.

"What? Why?"

Kelly's blue eyes darkened with tears. "Mom called to say Gran's not going to make it. We have to go say goodbye."

Hazel felt her stomach slide down to her toes. She forgot all about the motorcycle accident. Gran had been living in the long-term care ward for a while now, but the doctors thought she had more time.

"Get in," she said.

Hazel stuffed her secret shopping bag into her backpack and threw it into the backseat.

"Where were you?" Kelly demanded, rushing around the car. "I've been calling and calling. I ran all the way home from school! Why didn't you answer your phone?"

"I left it in Math, in that stupid phone bin," she said, cursing herself and her teacher's dumb policy. No one was allowed a phone in his class because he was afraid of cheating. "How long ago did Mom tell you?"

"45 minutes ago!" Kelly said, slamming the passenger door. Behind her anger there was fear.

Hazel put the car in reverse, stepped on the gas, and flew out of the driveway.

At the hospital, Hazel and Kelly ran up to Gran's room. They knew the way. When they arrived, their mom was just coming out of the room, wearing the usual green scrubs.

"She's asleep," Jolene said, wet eyes sparkling. "I-I don't think she's going to wake up again. You can go in, but be quiet."

She held the door for her daughters. Kelly burst into tears at the sight of Gran's limp form covered up to her chest in pale pink blankets. Hazel froze in shock on the threshold. The shadow stood triumphant at the foot of the bed. It looked more eerie than ever under the fluorescent lights. Hazel had never seen it leave Gran's house before. Jolene guided the girls closer, Hazel struggling not to resist. She reached out to take her grandmother's hand, one eye on the unwelcome guest. It was an effort to sense what little warmth was left in Gran's hand. Kelly laid her head on the blanket and cried.

Gran hung on for hours. Jolene, who was in and out of the room as much as her busy schedule allowed, informed them there was no clear reason for Gran's illness. She blamed it on old age, though Gran was only 70. Hazel threw hatred in the shadow's direction every time the grief threatened to overwhelm her. Its grin grew more pronounced as Gran weakened.

Towards dinner time, Jolene sent the girls home alone. She promised to call them when Gran passed away. The other nurses couldn't convince her to take the day off. Hazel knew staying busy was Jolene's way of coping, but both daughters cried as they walked away from their grandmother for the last time. Even so, the two sisters didn't say a word on the drive home. The only sounds that passed between them were muffled sniffs. When they closed the front door behind them, Hazel dragged her feet towards the kitchen.

"What do you want for dinner?" she asked in a monotone.

There was a creaking on the stairs and no reply. Kelly had fled to her room to cry. As soon as she was alone, Hazel's shoulders sagged and her face crumpled. She sunk into a kitchen chair and buried her face in her hands, the tears running down her palms. Her heart felt squeezed.

She had hoped Gran would get better when she was separated from the shadow and living in long-term care. Tonight it looked like somehow the thing had gone to her. It seemed to have been killing her all along, but Hazel couldn't see how. She felt a gnawing guilt. Maybe if she had said something, the doctors could have saved Gran.

The tears slowed as a disturbing thought occurred to Hazel. The shadow was bound to attach itself to someone else now. It was in a hospital full of already weakened patients that it could prey on. It might even come after Hazel, if it wanted to finish the job. She leaned back in her chair, old frustrations plaguing her again; if she told anyone, she risked being sent to a psych ward. If she told Riva, she risked her only real friend thinking she was crazy. If she told Kelly, Kelly would be petrified. If she told Jolene, Jolene would shut her down.

Hazel pressed her forehead to the cool wood table. She had come close to confessing once, at this very table. Years after the fight over Jessica, Kelly had asked Hazel at dinner if she remembered the girl who lived next door.

She had taken her time answering with a slow, "Yes..."

"I keep thinking about it," Kelly said, avoiding eye contact with Jolene as she played with her mashed potatoes. "So I asked the neighbours if they knew Jessica—," she pointed to the wall, on the other side of which were the neighbours who shared the duplex with them, "—and they said they bought the house off Jessica's parents when she died of leukemia. But Mom said they already owned the house when we started renting this side of the duplex." She shuddered. "So Jessica had already passed away when we moved in!"

"Kelly," Jolene sighed, but Kelly ignored her and pressed Hazel for more details.

Hazel filled her mouth with pork chops so she could delay responding. When she had to answer, she tried to stay vague. In the end, Jolene got fed up with the conversation and cut Kelly off.

"It's just a coincidence. Hazel has always had imaginary friends. Wait until you have kids, you'll see. It's normal," she gave her the stern look she was quick to give when switching from day shifts to nights. "Ghosts aren't real."

Hazel's mouth went dry and she couldn't swallow her food.

Her mom was wrong. The hope that one day Hazel could confide in her mother burst.

She let Kelly think the Jessica incident was a one-time event. Kelly carried on believing a ghost had shown itself to Hazel, not that Hazel could see ghosts all the time. Kelly was a chicken about paranormal stuff. She cried if anyone even suggested watching a scary movie. They had discovered this when Hazel went through what Jolene called her, "occult phase." By twelve, Hazel had devoured every scary movie, TV show, or book about hauntings or mediums that she could find. She scoured Reddit threads and worthless parts of the internet in search of something real. After a while she too started flinching at little noises and had to give it all up. Life as Hazel Conners was scary enough.

When her tears slowed, Hazel remembered the motorcycle accident. She abandoned the idea of dinner and went upstairs to find her laptop. It was on her twin bed, where she had tossed it that morning. In seconds she found an article that said a 27-year-old motorcyclist had been taken to the local hospital and was being treated for his injuries. She smiled. He wasn't dead. She had learned two skills from her internet searches: how to convince ghosts back into their bodies, and, more commonly, how to help them pass on. The motorcyclist was lucky enough to need only the first.

Leaning over to her nightstand, Hazel pulled out a thick, brown journal with a lock from her pre-laptop days. The leather was peeling away, revealing both how used it was and the fact that the leather was fake. As she pulled out the journal, she dislodged her bookmark, a pale blue collar belonging to her old cat. She paused and took the collar out of the drawer, wrapping it around her wrist as a bracelet. Salt had been protective in life, and Hazel thought she might need him tonight.

A sea shell sat next to the journal's resting place in the drawer. The sight of it reminded Hazel of her lunch-time shopping trip. She fished the new bundle of brittle, dried lavender out of her backpack. Whenever no one else was home, Hazel lit one end of the lavender braid and used the sea shell to catch the falling ash. She wafted the smoke around her room, and if she had time, around the rest of the house. It was another protective act. For some reason ghosts respected her space if she kept up with it.

The last time Hazel tried it, her mom came home and thought Hazel was smoking. Hazel hadn't managed to get further than her own room, and was too embarrassed to tell the truth. Jolene confiscated Hazel's car keys for a month. The ban ended last week, when Hazel snatched the proffered keys from her mother's hand. She headed straight to her car without a word, Jolene glowering at her back.

The journal was the one outlet Hazel had for her experiences with the dead. She had added all the details she could remember from her childhood, and now updated it after every visit. Hazel grabbed a black liquid-ink pen. She liked to use only nice pens in her journal. When she was finished she locked the journal back up and went downstairs to find a textbook.

She snuck a quick look into Kelly's room as she passed. Kelly had either fallen asleep on her stomach or was resting that way. Her phone was on the shelf she used as a nightstand. At least she would hear it buzz when Mom called to tell them about Gran. Sick at the thought, Hazel collected her textbook and promptly fell asleep studying.

She woke up with a jolt the next morning, realizing her phone was her alarm and her alarm was at school. She groaned and jerked upright, scooping her upside-down textbook off the floor to flatten the crumpled pages. She had been dreaming about the specters of the last 24 hours. She did a double-take at the door. Another stranger was standing in the doorway.

Lockdown

"Who are you?" she demanded, unsure if she was seeing a ghost or an intruder.

When Hazel saw a ghost, there was no transparency of the body. There was no glimmer that hinted she was in the presence of a soul. It was often only conversation that determined whether Hazel was speaking to a corporeal human or a ghost.

"What's happening?" the girl in the doorway asked. "What's happening?"

The girl looked only a few years older than Hazel. She was dithering at the threshold, wringing her hands but not entering. The lavender smoke had not worn off in Hazel's room yet. The question struck Hazel as odd, though. Ghosts usually asked why, not what.

"I'm guessing you died," she said, lowering her voice in case Kelly overheard. "I'm sorry."

"No," the girl said, and there was no denial in her voice, only fact. "My—my body..."

Hazel frowned. Most ghosts didn't grasp that they were out of their bodies right away.

"Can you tell me what happened to you?" Hazel asked, attempting a nonthreatening step closer.

"I have to go back!" the girl said, and she turned on her heel and ran.

"Wait!"

Hazel sped to the door and almost ran into Kelly.

"Whoa," Kelly said, "I'm not *going* anywhere. I was just coming to tell you Mom didn't come home last night. And she didn't call either. I tried her, but there was no answer."

Hazel stared at Kelly, uncomprehending. "You looked in her room?"

She headed down the hall, passing Kelly's room and the stairs.

"Obviously," Kelly said.

Hazel knocked on the open door and pushed it as she called, "Mom?"

The bed was immaculate and empty. She went to the master bathroom.

"Mom?"

It was empty too.

"Told you," Kelly said.

"She isn't downstairs?"

"See for yourself," Kelly replied.

Hazel went down the stairs two at a time, calling for Jolene. She wasn't in the kitchen at the front of the house, or the living room at the back. Hazel peeked out the blinds to see if she was in the backyard.

"Try her again," she said, worried now.

Kelly dialed as she returned to the kitchen, her overlong pajama pants brushing the carpet. It was Hazel's turn to follow at her heels.

"No answer," Kelly said after a minute.

Hazel groaned. "She probably left a message with me, but my phone is in the math bin."

"Why wouldn't she call me?"

"Maybe it was late and she didn't want to wake you. Try reception?"

Kelly went to the fridge, where the number was stuck up with a magnet.

"That's weird," Kelly said after a minute. "There's no answer at reception either."

"That is weird."

Hazel felt like she was missing her hand without her cellphone. Neither girl was willing to say aloud that Gran had died and Jolene needed them. Without confirmation, Hazel could not bring herself to believe that Gran was gone.

There was no guarantee that Gran would visit Hazel if she was dead. When Hazel's friend Riva lost her grandmother, there was no sign of the old woman. Hazel kept her eyes peeled, certain not to miss her dark skin amidst the sea of white faces in this town, but she never surfaced. Hazel supposed Riva's granny hadn't been confused about what to do next. Usually if a ghost did visit, they seemed confused. At least it had saved her having to explain herself to Riva.

"I'm going to get ready for school," Hazel announced. "We can try again after."

"You want to go to school? I thought, you know, under the circumstances..."

"I kind of have to if I want to check my phone."

"Oh," Kelly said, sagging with disappointment, "right."

* * *

They were running late by the time they got in Hazel's little black car. They were bickering about how long Hazel had taken in the shower. Kelly was pale and touchy, her hair unbrushed, and she had thrown on a pair of jeans and a t-shirt without the usual concern. Hazel had insisted they go to school on the pretense that Jolene wouldn't want them to miss a day. It was a flimsy, transparent reason, but Hazel thought Kelly might need the distraction.

"Promise me, if it's bad news we'll turn around and go home," Kelly said, and Hazel heard a tremor in her voice.

She felt a sting of guilt. "Fine."

They reached a four-way stop where a group of six were standing at the curb. Hazel paused to see which way they would cross, but none of them moved. They all looked at her with miserable morning faces.

"Okay..." she muttered, annoyed after a long wait.

Kelly didn't comment as Hazel drove on. She was staring at her phone and jiggling her foot.

The good parking lot at the front of the school was already packed from the Canada flag by the entrance to the chain-link fence by the road. They parked in the side lot of the school, where there were still spots left. Kelly's friend Di spotted them and ran to give Kelly a condolence hug. After a shy pause, she hugged Hazel too. Kelly and Di were in their first year of high school, grade 10, and had become fast friends. Di studied French ahead, so she and Hazel had a class together. She had wild, white-blonde curls and looked so delicate she made Hazel, who was already bigger than average, feel a little monstrous.

"Girls, let's go. First bell rang two minutes ago!" the principal called from the doorway. "Hazel, you missed wrestling practice this morning."

Hazel swore. Wrestling hadn't even been on her radar.

"Language!" he said.

"Sorry. We had a family emergency. I completely forgot."

His stern expression melted as he held the door for them. "Oh, is everything alright?"

Hazel shrugged, not sure what to say.

"Should I come with you to Math, first?" Kelly asked Hazel.

"I don't have Math first, I have French. I was going to stop in and grab my phone if there was time. I'll have to grab it at break." She avoided looking at Kelly as she sped off with Di, leaving her sister to explain things to the principal.

Hazel had a hard time concentrating in class. It wasn't just wondering where Jolene was, how Gran was, or what message might or might not be on her phone. There were people in the classroom who shouldn't have been there. The French room was on the top floor of the school, far down at the end of the hallway, with windows facing east and south. It wasn't a room people just stumbled into by accident. And these people in particular were not visible to anyone else.

Hazel had seen the odd ghost or two at school before. She could silence them with a look that said, "Not here, I'm busy." She tried the same with this group, but they seemed agitated. Three of them sat on the floor around her desk, whispering about an emergency until she plugged her ears, hands hiding under her hair. Two leaned against the door to wait, one biting her nails, the other checking the clock. Worst of all, one man wandered the room trying to get the attention of her classmates while tears trailed down his face. Hazel began to wonder about the group on the street corner, but the idea of so many new dead people in one morning made her sick with worry. Maybe Kelly would have seen the roadside group if she had looked up from her phone and proven them alive.

When the bell rang at last, Hazel muttered to the ghosts, "I have to get my phone from Math," gathered her books, and was the first out the door.

On the first floor she joined the throng of students already heading to their lockers. Then a scream erupted over the chatter. All heads turned towards the lobby at the west end of the school.

"You think someone's fighting?" a girl asked her friend. The two exchanged anxious looks, then joined the stream heading towards the commotion in the lobby.

Hazel bobbed along behind them, needing to cross through the jabbering students to get to the South wing. Then there was more screaming, and this time it was many voices, the pitch too high to be a joke. Breathing in the hallway stopped. There was some pushback in the flow of students. The principal's voice sounded over the P.A. system.

"Lockdown, lockdown, lockdown!" he yelled into the phone.

The P.A. magnified the screaming so that the voices were coming from the speakers all around them. The sound was so horrifying that Hazel's eyes prickled. Then the principal screamed too, and Hazel stood, petrified, behind the girls who had hoped to see a fight.

Ms. Burrough appeared at the door of her social studies classroom and hollered over the screams, "Get inside the nearest class! Now! Move! Let's go, let's go! No pushing!"

Hazel wheeled around. Her classmates were scattering, pushing past one another in different directions. She was sure half of them hadn't heard Ms. Burrough's instructions. Her shoulder collided with someone and she spun full circle. There were logjams of students at every door.

She ran for the stairs, where the way was clear, and bolted up, skipping two at a time like she always did at home. Visions of guns and violence flashed in her mind, and every step echoed, *Kelly, Kelly, Kelly.* There were fewer people in the upstairs hallway, and doors were already slamming shut. A shadow peered out of the French classroom opposite Hazel, and she almost missed a step, but then Hazel recognized the long, angular eyebrows at odds with round, dark cheekbones.

"Hazel!" Riva said, waving her over.

When she was close enough, Riva grabbed her arm and yanked her inside. Riva stayed at the door, eyes still darting around to see if everyone had somewhere safe to go. Hazel counted the rest of the students. There were only five, plus herself and Riva. The ghosts had left.

"Where is everyone? Where's Mr. Auberg?" she asked.

Di, who was closing all the shutters with a switch on the back wall, whispered, "Keep your voice down."

Someone at the back of the room answered, "A couple of the girls went to the washroom when the bell went." It was Alexis, a grade 11 student in a short, flared skirt who Hazel barely knew. She was sitting on a low bookshelf as far from the door as she could get. She looked around at her classmates for input, black, high-backed sneakers dangling. "I think Mr. Auberg must have gone to the staffroom?"

Another grade 11, Breanna, had her hands over her ears. She whispered, "I know a bunch of them are supposed to have P.E. next block, on the other side of the school." She chewed her lip for a moment, then pressed harder on her ears. "Why is the P.A. still on? I can't take it!"

There were fewer voices screaming now. Hazel tried to remember what class Kelly had first, or where in the school she might be. She stopped trying to block out the screaming for a moment and strained to hear if Kelly's voice was among them. Her whole body went cold with the effort.

Riva shut the door as if the smallest click would set off a bomb.

"What about the others?" asked Alexis.

"Mrs. Jimmy signaled she wanted me to shut it," Riva said, running a hand over her thick braids to make sure they were all collected in a ponytail. Her hair was short enough that the ends of the braids stuck straight out from her head.

Riva grabbed a class list off Mr. Auberg's desk. They gathered around a desk to pour over it, marking themselves down and guessing where their missing members might be. Hazel, Di, Alexis, Breanna, and Jen and Morgan were all who were present out of twenty-five class members. Riva had taken refuge in the open room on her way between Socials and English. A few of the students started texting to check on their missing friends. As Riva added her name to the bottom of the list, Jen met Hazel's eyes across the desk. Hazel's stomach flipped. Embarrassed, she dropped her gaze to the tiny diamond stud on Jen's left nostril instead.

"Are your messages getting through?" Morgan whispered, one hand holding up her phone, the other twisting a long gold necklace.

Alexis shook her head. "No reply. What's going on out there?" She crept to the door to listen, her blonde ponytail swaying.

"Do you hear anything?"

"More screaming," she said, and her voice cracked, "but it's not from the lobby."

"Who's doing this?" Breanna asked, panicking. "Who would come to school with a-a gun?"

Morgan started naming some students she found suspicious from atop her desk, but Breanna defended each of them. Hazel went to her usual spot and sat in the chair, unable to think of anything except her sister. Jen raised the shutters an inch and made a crack in the blinds. She was wearing jean shorts and a hot pink t-shirt that showed her natural athletic build. She had bronze skin inherited from Mexican parents, and long, dark, purposefully loose curls.

"I see people out there," Jen said.

"Police?" Morgan jumped up to join her, a blur of black hair, she moved so fast.

At the same time, three ghosts re-entered the room. Hazel stood up, torn between getting answers from them and checking on rescue at the window.

"I don't know," Jen said, oblivious to the newcomers, "but they look... They look like they're covered in blood."

Everyone except Alexis, whose ear was still pressed to the door, gathered at the window. The plastic blinds crackled as they each found a spot. Down below, people meandered across the sunny front lawn. Jen was right. There were red throats, red hands, red mouths, and red guts.

"It's a joke, right?" Jen asked at last, watching their slow, almost casual progress. "A zombie-joke?"

"Oh," Morgan sighed, the quickest to cling to a logical answer. "Yeah, I haven't heard any gunshots!"

The rest of the group watched in doubtful silence. Hazel looked to the ghosts. Two of them shook their heads. Hazel couldn't believe the school would allow a joke like this to happen. The lockdown was traumatizing enough without bloody figures in the field below. She needed to ask the ghosts some questions without being noticed.

"Look it up," Breanna suggested, raising her own phone.

The P.A. had gone quiet, but no one dared comment.

Finally Breanna said, "Something happened at the hospital

last night."

"What?" Hazel demanded. She felt dizzy. It was overwhelming, worrying about every family member in different places and different dangers all at once.

A scream echoed down the hall. They all froze. There were crashes, shouts, then more screams. The ghosts tensed as much as the students. Whatever was happening had reached their floor. Hazel tip-toed to the east windows to pretend to look out over the empty side-yard.

She whispered to a slim man with a bushy beard, "How did you die?"

The man began to cry. Hazel waited, but he couldn't get out anything sensible. She looked to an old woman with no hair.

"I thought it would be the cancer," the bald woman said. "I spent so much time worrying about it. What a waste."

Riva, Di, and Alexis had their hands over their mouths as they listened to the commotion in the halls. Breanna was crying, Jen shaking. Morgan paced the back of the room.

"It was a monster," the old woman said, and she started to cry too. "It came into my room growling like a dog."

"There's hundreds of them," a woman with wide, frightened eyes added. "Five tackled me in the stairwell. They...ate me."

Hazel's hands went cold. "What-what are they?"

"People," the sobbing man choked. "People."

"I had visions," the old woman said. "They made me have terrible visions."

The other two nodded. There was banging outside in the hallway, coming closer.

"Oh my god," Di whispered, pulling her giant, beige knit cardigan tighter over her chest.

"The other people in the hospital?" Hazel asked, her throat

dry.

"What?" Jen asked.

"I-I said I think we should hide," Hazel lied.

The only real spot was under the teacher's heavy desk, beside the door. The girls moved to hide behind it. Hazel threw the ghosts an urgent stare.

"I think they're all dead," the younger woman whispered.

Hazel bit her lip. She couldn't entertain the idea of her mom being dead. It was a struggle just to accept that Gran was gone. But the woman with cancer was standing right beside Hazel, alive this morning, and now dead.

"Hazel!" Riva hissed from behind the desk.

Hazel hastened to join them, but made it no further than halfway when Kelly burst in, sobbing.

"Hazel!" she cried, and threw her arms around her sister.

Somehow she collapsed on the floor behind Hazel.

"No," Hazel whispered, and the cold of her hands was nothing compared to the ice in her bones. The door had not opened.

"What?" Riva asked.

There was a bang on the door and the whole group in the French room cried out in shock.

Kelly cowered on the floor and begged, "Block the door! Don't let them in here!"

Hazel pulled her leg from the ground as if it was stuck in quicksand. She ran to the desk, sluggish and heavy, and whispered, "Push!"

The girls shoved the desk up against the door and then backed away as the banging went on.

"It's a sturdy door," Alexis said.

There was a snarling from the hallway.

"Dogs?" Breanna asked, eyes bulging.

"Get out of here, Hazel!" Kelly sobbed.

Hazel took her advice. "Riva, open the shutters, I'll get the window!"

Hazel ran to the east window. She yanked up the blinds with a buzzing clatter. It was an excruciating wait for the shutters to open enough. She pulled back the locks and shoved the window up, looking down at the concrete awning over the side door and the grass in the deserted yard below.

"That's not too bad," Riva said, joining her.

"We don't know if it's safe out there either," Jen added from Hazel's other side.

The door rattled on its hinges with the next bang, and the doorknob jolted. The door opened a crack.

"It's not locked," Riva gasped.

Alexis lunged over the desk and grabbed the handle. She leaned back as far as she could to use her body weight. She didn't look like much, slight as she was, but the other girls backed away, too frightened to help.

"Let's go!" Hazel said.

"Lock it, Alexis!" Breanna cried.

"I can't! There are fingers in the crack!" Alexis shrieked.

On the other side, there was a horrible, low scream as the fingers began to bleed.

"Who's going first?" Hazel asked, willing someone else to volunteer.

Jen came forward, ill with fright. She climbed the low bookshelf, stuck her legs out the window, and ducked her head out. She paused, looking down at the ground, trying to assess the best way to jump.

"If you grab the window sill and dangle, you'll be closer to the awning," Riva suggested, her head out the window as well.

"I can't do this!" Alexis screamed from the door.

Hazel glanced back and saw more fingers in the crack, fighting against Alexis. Most of them were dripping red.

"Go!" she yelled at Jen.

Jen threw herself out the second-story window and fell. They heard a thump.

"Are you okay?" Riva called down.

Jen put her thumb and index finger together, giving them the 'perfect' signal from the awning. Breanna went to help Alexis with the door, shaking all the way.

"She's fine," Riva said as Jen climbed off the awning. She grabbed Morgan by her striped shirt and guided her to the window.

"Look out!" Morgan called down as she scrambled up the bookshelf.

The door slipped from Alexis and Breanna's hands. They both fell backwards. In the hallway were their classmates, each of them baring bloody teeth. At the forefront was a girl Hazel knew from middle school. She was trailing sausage-like intestines out of her torso. As she crawled over the desk, blood splashed from her gaping stomach as if tipped from a slop bucket. The others threw themselves past her, shoving each other in their rush to get in.

Riva pushed Morgan out the window as Alexis screamed in terror. Without thinking, Hazel seized a desk and flung it with all her might at the monsters about to set upon Alexis. They went down like bowling pins and Alexis scrambled backwards, Breanna dragging her to her feet.

Hazel grabbed desk after desk and kept hurling them at the door. Her muscles burned from abs to biceps, but she ignored them, Kelly's screams to run faint in her ears. The ghosts abandoned them, unable to face another massacre. Breanna had pushed Alexis ahead of her and the two were leaping and swinging over the remaining desks in a race to the window. The rabid students got back up and stumbled after the two girls, licking their lips. Hazel had to choose between defending the door or her two classmates.

She groaned as she threw another desk and took down a boy she recognized from P.E as he clawed at the girls. The desks were getting heavier as Hazel wore out. The girl she knew from middle school seized Breanna's long ponytail. Breanna went down backwards with a crash, screaming. The girl buried her teeth in her throat and twisted back and forth, blood spattering from her own stomach. Alexis screamed in horror as she hurtled towards the window. Several more students fell upon Breanna, buying Alexis another second to hurl herself out.

"Hazel, go!" Riva yelled, seizing her arm and swinging her around.

Hazel scrambled up onto the ledge with the feeling that she was abandoning Breanna. The escaped girls on the grass below were waving and shouting for her to jump. With an effort, she swung her legs out, ducked her head, and pushed off. She met with a rush of wind that didn't block out Breanna's dying gurgles. The awning shook as it took her weight. She didn't pause before clambering over the edge. Her heel hit the ground first, then she thumped onto her back.

Jen pulled her to her feet to make room for Riva, a jolt of pain still running a zig-zag from Hazel's heel to her calf. Riva screamed and Hazel felt all the blood in her face slip away. Her hands clutched her cheeks. The zombies were climbing out the window after them.

Run

“Oh god, oh god, Breanna!” Alexis gasped, still grasping the loss and how close she had come to death.

Hazel realized she herself had huge tears pouring over her eyelids and fingers.

“Hazel!” Kelly called, no longer in the window, but beside her.

One of the figures Hazel had seen from the window had rounded the corner and spotted them. It was a man in a paramedic's uniform. Like the students upstairs, his mouth was stained and his throat was gaping. He broke into a run.

“Look out!” she yelped to her classmates.

She turned on her heel and bolted towards the back field. The others followed. As they rounded the corner, Hazel saw the field was littered with more monsters. In the far right corner there was a former barn that housed an auto shop for the mechanics students. The path there was clear. Hazel beelined towards it.

Not for the first time, Hazel was glad that she was fast, could run long distances, and best of all, that no one ever expected she could. She loved to break out the element of surprise to show everyone that she was more than just her weight. She went for runs most mornings around her neighbourhood. Today, it could keep her alive. She pushed herself so that her arms and legs were pumping harder than ever. She ignored that she had no sports bra or running shoes, and let her ballet flats fly off her feet. The breath and stomping of her classmates soon fell behind.

The monsters in the field all ran towards her. They didn't run slow; they moved like cheetahs after prey. One of them was ahead of Hazel on her left. Twenty feet from him, Hazel swerved to the right and skirted the growling monster. He closed the gap. Hazel screwed up her face as she forced herself to outstrip him. With the morning sunlight, dandelions growing in the grass, and her bare feet, it was like playing tag as a kid. Only Hazel couldn't tell if her heart or her feet were beating faster. She could hear him growling as she pushed on, nearing the two garage doors of the auto shop.

On her right was the chain-link fence that separated the shop and field from neighbouring houses. Hazel chanced a glance over her shoulder and realized her classmates couldn't make it to the garage. Half of them were already clambering over the fence as their pursuers closed in. She cursed and darted to the chain-link. She threw herself onto the fence as high as she could, sweeping over the top with only one more step. Legs on the other side, she had a terrifying glimpse of the monster face-to-face with her. She recognized him from science class. She stumbled backwards out of harm's way.

There was a scream to her left. Alexis was lying where she had fallen, crawling backwards as a zombie swiped at her feet and two more rattled the chain-link, climbing after her. These were not the zombies Hazel knew from TV, who were hindered by a little fence. Jen was still dodging monsters in the school field, all too close to catching her for any escape over the fence. She was running circles and faking left and right, but they were only getting nearer. The monster in front of Hazel leapt onto the fence, snapping at her face. Riva was racing to Alexis' side, her own pursuers hitting the fence, so Hazel chose Jen.

She ran down the fence, away from her science classmate and climbed back over just as he made it to the neighbourhood side. In her head, she counted out her breath to calm the call of panic in her chest. She stretched it out to the count of four. Then she put on a burst of speed with the nearest monster in her sights. Hazel seized him around the waist and flung him to the ground. Her head was full of her wrestling training, and she backed off, switching from offensive to defensive before the monster could grab her. Over her shoulder, she saw that all but the monster closest to Jen had turned their eyes to her. If they were anything like their former selves, they might assume Hazel was a slow target.

She ran into the middle of the field, and the monsters ran after her. She circled back so that she was following Jen, who was taking the opportunity to race to the fence. The monster from science was now bearing down on Riva and Alexis as they climbed a tree. Other monsters were climbing the tree too, showing just as much skill as their living counterparts. With equal parts fear and relief, Hazel saw Morgan's feet pumping and Di's frizzy white hair flying towards the girls.

Jen reached the fence. Even as she scaled it, the monster chasing her caught up and grabbed her around the waist, sinking its teeth into her hip. Jen screamed in pain and terror.

Hazel lunged at the monster, grabbing it by the hair and yanking its head back so hard it released its bite. Jen flipped to the safer side of the fence and landed on her back with a painful thump. She rolled away from the fence, fingers red from clutching her wound.

With a handful of the monster's hair, Hazel swung it around at arms-length, blocking the other monsters from reaching her. She shoved it into their path and turned on her heel once again, but it was too close to risk climbing the fence. For the first time she realized just how near death she was, and it made her squint against the unusually brilliant jade of the grass and the over-bright sky. Jen ran alongside her, the chain-link separating them. Hazel spotted her sister there too.

She sprinted into the skinny gap between the auto shop and the fence. The monsters piled in after each other, and Hazel's breaths came short with panic. Hair flying out behind her, she leapt over rocks and litter. Jen was falling behind in her flimsy white sandals, and would soon become a target if the monsters realized it.

"Jen!" she panted. "Loop around a house and go back to the others!"

"But—"

"I'm faster than you!" she insisted.

Jen cursed, and Hazel knew it had dawned on her what being the slower meal meant. She sensed Jen swerve to the right. Relieved, Hazel rounded the corner of the building and her feet slapped crumbling pavement. The corner bought her a little more time and she pulled ahead. There was a door on this side too. She seized the handle and pushed, but it didn't budge. Advantage lost, she was forced to spin around the next corner, arching her back to avoid the clutching hands after her. In seconds she would be back to the side of the building with the garage doors. Her last hope was the door next to them.

Bits of gravel on the road jabbed into her feet and made her cry out. More of the rabid students were in the field running towards her. Rounding the last corner, she made it to the door.

She slammed into it and it burst open. To her dismay, there was a key hole on both side of the handle; it needed a key to lock it. All the doors in the school were the same. She cursed and slammed it shut, then cast around the pitch-black room, inhaling the strong odor of metal and oil. On the wall opposite were stairs leading up to a half-loft left over from the building's days as a barn.

She dashed around the two junk cars the students had been working on, each facing one of the garage doors, and hesitated. Both had their windows open, but it might take too long to roll them up. She kept going for the stairs. Two at time, she made it to the top and dropped to her stomach, spinning to face the door and trying to blend into the darkness. The door banged back open and the building erupted with echoing growls. A small gasp beside her made Hazel flinch, but it was only Kelly, still at her side.

The desperate hunger on the faces below sent a chill though Hazel. The monsters licked their lips as their eyes flashed around the dark auto shop. They shoved tool chests out of their way, the contents clanging together before crashing to the cement floor, deafening. Others crowded the cars, leering inside or swiping underneath. They were so many they were getting in each other's way. Just as Hazel decided she could chance searching for a weapon, her eyes fell on one of the monsters. Kelly gasped.

From the front, Kelly's body looked almost intact. Only her shoulders were torn, the blood dripping in long streams down her bare arms. Her blue eyes had the hollow look she sometimes got when she hadn't had enough to eat. When Kelly ducked to swipe under the nearest car, Hazel felt the prickle of hair rising on her arms. She didn't move like Kelly. It was like someone else had taken over.

The movement gave Hazel a clear view of her sister's back. The black t-shirt she had thrown on this morning was torn in ribbons and sticking to a mess of chunky flesh and stripped ribs. The worst wound was above her left hip, the same place Jen had been bitten. The blood that remained in her body glugged out like syrup. It was almost black, and it painted Kelly's jeans from pocket to hem. Hazel gagged and slapped a hand to her mouth.

The Kelly beside her attempted to grab a handful of Hazel's shirt, but overbalanced when they couldn't interact.

"I can't— I can't— I can't—," Kelly stuttered, and she pointed at her mangled body, hand shaking.

Hazel got the message. Kelly couldn't bear to witness herself tearing into her sister's flesh with her teeth, ignoring Hazel's screams until they stopped forever. The hyper-awareness that had lit up Hazel's world while she ran to save herself shattered like a glass cup. Out poured the fear she had trapped inside it. She swallowed to control her voice.

"You don't have to," she offered.

What little light reached them lit the tears in Kelly's eyes. She shook her head. Hazel bit her lip and lowered her gaze to their hands. They were inches apart, but they would never touch again.

"I don't want to die," she whispered, and she despised herself for saying so after what Kelly had just been through.

Kelly glanced around the loft as Hazel listened to the snarling below. "We have to find you a weapon, or a way out."

Too afraid to sniff, Hazel wiped her nose on her cardigan and backed away from the edge. The floorboards creaked under her knees. Piled in the back corner of the loft were boxes of tools and car parts. All the boxes were heavy.

"Can you block the stairs?" Kelly asked.

Hazel lifted a box of scrap parts, but the tape that held the box together was old and dry. The box tore and metal tumbled over her arm, clanking and thumping to the wooden floor. Kelly ran to the stairs.

"They heard," she confirmed, as Hazel juggled the box.

With most of the contents gone, Hazel hefted the box over her head and hurled it in the direction of the stairs. It soared over the edge, spewing the rest of its contents on the monsters below.

Kelly snorted and called over her shoulder, "George is grabbing his head. You smoked him with a tire iron."

Hazel grabbed the next box, determined to keep going until there were none left.

"I feel bad now," Kelly admitted. "George is an ass, but he didn't deserve to die."

Hazel wasn't listening. She shoved her emotions into a box in her mind and concentrated on action. The next box hit the stairs at an angle and bounced lethally.

"Got one! They're hesitating now. Hold on, I'll tell you when."

Hazel positioned the next box on her shoulder. She could feel it shifting as the old tape started to crack.

"Now!"

This time there was a scream. Hazel hurried to the edge to see for herself. The monsters were crowded around the narrow stairs, trying to push each other into the line of fire. The girl who had screamed was lying in a heap at the foot of the stairs, sprawled over the box. Hazel had smashed her head in over the left eye.

"I think you killed her," Kelly said.

They stared at the motionless figure, hoping it was indeed possible to kill someone who was already dead. Then the girl shifted and crawled back to her feet, dazed by the blow, but not dead. Hazel and Kelly exchanged a glance. Hazel ran for another box.

As the morning went on, the zombies trickled back out of the auto shop. A few continued to wait below, pacing the ground floor, but not daring to climb the stairs. Hazel had nothing to do. Around noon, her stomach growled and she could understand giving up on such an uncooperative meal. Kelly's body had left too. The girls were giddy with relief. Hazel was not going to die at her sister's hands, and there was a way to fight back. The zombies might not die, but they didn't seem to like pain or hunger any more than their victims.

Hazel fiddled with another rusty four-spoked tire iron she had saved as a weapon, spinning it around on her palm. "Where do you think Riva and them went? Do you think they got away?"

Kelly was quiet for a moment. "Should I check? Can I check?"

Kelly was asking for Hazel's experienced opinion. Hazel froze for a moment. She didn't know how to feel. Someone finally knew about her abilities, but the cost had been so high.

"Yeah," Hazel answered, not meeting Kelly's eye. "I mean, there are limits to how far from your body you can go, but it's pretty wide."

Kelly got to her feet without another word and descended the steps. She passed through the two remaining monsters with a cringe, but paused at the door.

"Do you know about Gran? Or Mom?"

Hazel neared the edge enough to shake her head at Kelly. Kelly frowned with worry.

"I'll be right back," she said. "Be careful."

Twenty minutes passed, and the last two monsters finally gave up. They left through the still open door. Hazel teetered on the verge of climbing down. She didn't want to lose Kelly. If she travelled beyond Kelly's limits, they might never cross paths again. The thought made her breath catch in her chest. Then there was the problem of what was out there. Hazel could be exposing herself to wandering zombies. Plus, this was the last place Jen knew she was headed. If the girls were coming back for her it would be stupid to leave.

Hazel stared at the bright slice of grass she could see through the door. She had been making so much noise before she hadn't noticed the growling and screaming stop. Panic hit her. Maybe the others were dead. She might already be alone. She had a powerful urge to go home, where she felt safe. If the monsters had swept in from the right, west, that meant her house, being between the hospital and the school, was off limits.

Clutching the tire iron, she padded down the stairs to the door and stuck her head out into the blinding sunlight. One or two maimed zombies were stumbling around in the neighbouring yard where Riva, Di, Morgan, and Alexis had fought them off. At least, she hoped they had fought them off. With any luck, Jen had joined the girls and they were somewhere safe now, all together.

Looking right, Hazel could see her car in the distance. She had abandoned her keys along with her bag at the school. She looked up at the long, two-story building, and wondered if anyone was alive in there. She tried to catch sight of eyes peering through the blinds, but if anyone was watching to see if Hazel Conners was still alive, she couldn't tell. It would be stupid to go back in there, she decided. She had to go east after Kelly and her classmates, into the neighbourhood where they had vanished.

Hazel shut the door. She grappled along the wall until she found a light switch. The hum of fluorescent lights filled the room as they flickered on. Hazel stared at the two cars. If they worked, she could take one. She ran to the first car, and stuck her head in the window. There were no keys. She tried the second, stepping over the mess of tools. Again, none. The windows were open, so the shop teacher wasn't concerned with thieves. Hazel grabbed at the sun visor and pulled it down. With a jingle, key and keychain plunked to the floor.

"Yes!" she gasped.

It was a beige 1980's Nissan Pulsar, still clinging to life. The paint was peeling and horizontal black stripes ran down the sides. She opened the door and grabbed the keys, then stood back, thinking. She would need to open the noisy garage door and get back in the car before any zombies caught her. She wondered if it would even start. Hazel sat behind the wheel, heart racing.

With a jolt she saw Breanna standing in front of the car. She froze, waiting for an attack.

Drive

"Do up the windows," Breanna advised.

Hazel let out a breath of relief. "Thanks."

She leaned across the passenger seat and cranked the pump that rolled it up. When she finished, she looked across at Breanna again. She was standing in the same spot, one brown braid stretching from her forehead to her high ponytail, as perfect as it had been this morning. She had low, round cheeks and tiny lips that gave her face a glum expression. In her shorts, flip-flops, and lavender sweater, she looked too young for her fate, like Jessica had been all those years ago.

"Are-are you getting in?"

"You should block the door. In case the car doesn't start, but it attracts attention."

"Right."

She did as Breanna said, finding an upended tool cabinet that was heavy enough to buy her some time. It was painstaking work, shoving its emptied contents out of the way and trying to push it across the floor without making any noise. Breanna watched with a somber expression that made Hazel uncomfortable.

She got back in the car and gripped the keys, nerves taut. "So...are you coming?"

Breanna continued to stare at her.

"I–I'd like you to come," Hazel said.

Breanna didn't move. Hazel tried to fight back the sinking feeling in her stomach. She felt in part to blame for Breanna's death, and the fact was now staring her in the face with that glum expression.

"I'm sorry," she choked, unable to bear it.

"For what?" Breanna asked, and her voice was hard.

"F–for not saving you," she said, tears dancing over her lower lids.

"I'm not dead," Breanna said in a dangerous, low tone. "I'm standing right in front of you."

For a second Hazel second-guessed her assumption, but she had encountered denial in ghosts before. She said what she usually did, and following the familiar words helped her toughen up against the guilt.

"A lot of people are dead today," she began. "Which means they aren't connected to their bodies, or living things, any more. It doesn't mean they're gone yet. I'm an exception. They can interact with me, but not physically." She paused to see how Breanna was taking this. She looked defensive. "You can try to touch me, if you want."

"I don't want to," she snapped. "I don't need to."

"If you really believed that, you'd be in this car, getting out of here."

Breanna threw her a scathing look.

"Look, I want to help you," Hazel said. "I owe you. But I have to get out of here. Please come with me. Please, Breanna?"

Breanna glared elsewhere for a moment, then said, "Oh, fine!"

She made a motion like she was opening the passenger door,

but in reality she just slipped through. It was like how Kelly had taken the stairs. As ghosts they didn't need to, but it was how they thought the world worked.

"Okay," Hazel said, and she turned the key so that the lights came on.

A further turn of the key revved the engine, but it didn't catch. Hazel cursed. She tried again. Getting the idea from her own car, Hazel turned the key and hit the gas, putting the car into drive as fast as she could. The car lurched forward, but died when she hit the brakes. It might work.

"The noise," Breanna reminded her.

"I know."

Heart hammering, Hazel got out and found the garage door opener on the wall. She pushed the button and ran back to the car, slamming the door behind her. She turned the key, hit the gas, and threw the car into drive. It lurched forward again and this time she let it drift forward as the door raised up.

"Come on," she urged both the car and the door.

She kept her eyes on the growing crack, watching for zombie-feet. It raised to the hood of the little Nissan, which started to slide under. If it didn't clear the roof she would have to hit the brakes and lose time restarting the car. Sunlight drifted up her body as the door raised. Her eyes adjusted to the light as a hand banged down on the hood, or it would have if Kelly had been in her physical form. She ducked under the door and got in the backseat.

"Aren't you Breanna Kent?" she asked the other passenger in surprise.

"Hey," Breanna replied.

Both girls looked around awkwardly, not sure what to say next. Hazel didn't have time for the small talk of the dead. The top of the windshield was almost touching the door, and the zombies outside had noticed both the noise and the movement. The ones across the fence were running towards them, while those across the field were also starting to show interest.

The car hit the door. It was so close that Hazel chanced it and didn't touch the brake. There was a grinding scrape, and then they were clear. Hazel punched the gas. The car flew out of the garage and she cranked the steering wheel so they swung to the right. The zombies reached the fence and clambered over. Breanna moaned as she watched them sprinting through the rear-view mirror.

Hazel kept the wheel cranked until the school itself was in the rear-view. The tires squealed on the broken pavement. With zombies closing in on both passenger and driver's sides, Hazel was clear to speed away. She fired towards the road at the end of the field.

"You did it!" Kelly cheered.

"I don't know where I'm going," Hazel said, tense.

"Go right at the end of the field," Kelly said. "The others are breaking into a neighbour's shed for weapons. I'll show you where."

There were no other cars on the road as they drove down the backstreet. Even the houses looked empty, but then it was a Tuesday in the middle of the day. Most people were either at school or work. Hazel kept her eyes peeled. Zombies were already wandering gardens, growling at the car as they passed. They were being trailed in the distance by a pack of five who were not tiring out. One of them was Mr. Auberg. Hazel tried to keep the speed above fifty to lose them.

"Right, ahead," Kelly said.

Hazel let the car glide to the corner and turned wide but fast.

She had to jerk the wheel to avoid a parked car. The houses here were set behind short front yards.

"They should be here. They were behind that yellow house, can you see into the backyard?"

Hazel slowed just enough to see an open shed before the house blocked her view. No one was there.

"Try the next block."

They rounded the corner and went up the parallel road.

"There's people here," Breanna said, worried. "We should warn them."

"I don't think they're people," Hazel reassured her.

She noticed the way they watched her go by. In this town it was normal to receive a glare of reproach for speeding in a residential area; these people were observing the car's progress with sad expressions. There was still no sign of the girls. She turned down the next block.

"There!" Breanna cried, and Hazel spotted Morgan's black-and-white striped shirt.

The girls were retreating behind a tall wooden gate. She braked hard.

"Hazel!" Riva squealed with the brakes.

The car stopped and died. Hazel tried to restart it, but this time the lights were dim.

"No, no, no," she said. "Don't die! You were fine, come on!"

She turned the key again, but the engine didn't even turn over. The lights went out as the zombies bore down on car and the girls rushed towards her from the yard.

Weapons

"No, go back!" she yelled, cutting their celebrations short. "Go back!"

She ditched the car in the middle of the road, slamming the door out of habit.

"It died!" she shouted as she joined them. "Run!"

She dashed through the middle of the group and led them through the gate into the backyard. The latch clicked behind them. Hazel glanced around, looking for the next escape. There was a trampoline in one corner, a small shed in the other, and a wheelbarrow left out beside a rose bush.

"The fence is tall," Di reasoned, her pale face flushed from running.

"I'll try the door," said Alexis, who was closest to the back porch.

Meanwhile, Jen jumped at the back fence to look into the next yard. There was blood on Jen's shirt where her hip had been bitten.

"Locked," Alexis said. She was carrying a pair of gardening shears.

Riva dropped the rake she was carrying and yanked at the branch of a tree next to the house. She twisted and snapped a thick twig off, which she stuffed through the latch on the gate as a make-shift lock. At that moment there was a bang as one of the zombies threw itself into the fence.

"Jen?" Riva called over her shoulder.

"It's more of the same," Jen said, shaking her head. Her dark curls were going flat. "The fences are going to slow all of us down."

It was one thing to get a toehold in a chain-link fence, and another to scale a wooden one. Without a trampoline in every yard, they would have a hard time climbing. Hazel caught Morgan giving her a critical look. She jerked her gaze away when she caught Hazel's eye, pretending she was still searching for an escape. Hazel felt a blush of anger cross her cheeks.

"We can make them back off," Hazel said. "In the auto shop I threw stuff at them until they gave up."

"Yeah, and the helicopter shot those ones in the trees and they ran," Di said.

"Helicopter?" Kelly asked her friend. No one but Hazel heard her.

"Hazel, see if you can find a weapon in the shed," Morgan spoke over her, eyeing the pathetic tire iron in her hand. "And someone help me block the gate with this trampoline."

Alexis defended the gate with her gardening shears, slicing at any fingers that managed to grab the top. Everyone else grabbed a leg of the trampoline while Hazel ran to the shed. There, she found a combination lock on the door. She tugged at it, but it didn't budge. Other than the wheelbarrow, there was nothing lying around. She reached inside the wheelbarrow and tossed aside a pair of gardening gloves. Underneath them was a small trowel. It would have to do.

A weapon in each hand, she jogged back to the girls. Alexis slid out of the way as they pushed the trampoline against the gate.

"Who's got the best weapon?" Morgan asked.

"I've got an arm's length," Riva said, lifting her rake.

"These shears are sharp," Alexis added as she tied tight double-knots in her high-backed sneakers.

They looked at the rest of the gardening equipment: a hoe with an arm as long as the rake, but ending in a sharp little triangle on a hook; a shovel; a hand-sized cultivator with three prongs; and the pathetic trowel and tire iron. Alexis, with the shears, and Jen, with the gardening hoe, climbed onto the trampoline to beat back their pursuers.

Morgan and Riva waited on the ground, weapons at the ready, knuckles white. Hazel and Di tried the windows of the house to no avail. Then a horrible scream interrupted from the other side of the fence and they rushed back to see Alexis doubled-over on the trampoline, vomiting.

Still wielding the hoe, Jen gagged and said, "Alexis stabbed one in the eye."

Riva vaulted up to take Alexis' place, scooping up the shears.

"Wait," Hazel said, "if they can't see us..."

With one look of agreement, Riva and Jen switched from whacking to stabbing. There were more screams.

"Alexis, get out of here," Jen said as puke rolled across the black fabric to her feet.

Hazel moved fastest, desperate to help. She swept around the trampoline to take Alexis' arm. She was shaking and cold to the touch.

"It was Mr. Auberg," Alexis choked, the edge of her skirt catching on a spring.

Hazel grimaced and pulled the fabric free. "Don't think of it that way. He's not himself anymore."

Alexis jumped down and Hazel led her to the porch stairs.

"How do you know that?" Di asked, trailing after them. Her hands tensed and twisted on her cultivator, and there was a pleading note in her voice. "Maybe they're just sick. Maybe they can get better."

"I can't see what's going on," Morgan said, agitated. She climbed onto the trampoline to get a better view, staying well back from the other two.

"They're not sick," Hazel said, sitting down with Alexis on the steps.

"Did you hear something?" Di asked, a dead girl on each side of her. "Was there something on the radio?"

"No. I–I just know."

"How?"

Hazel cast around for an answer that didn't include the phrase, "I see dead people."

"Me," Kelly supplied.

It took Hazel a moment to understand.

"My sister is dead."

Di gasped. Hazel cringed. She had forgotten Di and Kelly were so close. She wished she hadn't been so blunt, but it didn't feel real anymore.

"No..." Di breathed.

"Her body attacked me," Hazel said, trying to be gentler. "Kelly would never do that to me. No matter how sick."

Di sunk to the ground, her face obscured by messy, white curls. Alexis buried her face in her hands. Hazel couldn't look at her sister to see how she was taking her best friend's reaction. She locked eyes with Breanna instead, who was standing stock-still, absorbing the fact that she, too, was dead too.

"I can't do this anymore," Jen called, and they all looked up to see her switch with Morgan.

She jumped off the trampoline and joined them, looking as ill as Alexis.

"They took over the school really fast," Hazel said, her mind still whirring. "What if more are coming this way?"

"We can't stay outside," Alexis said, tightening the laces of her black shoes again, as if that was the whole reason for sitting down. She clapped her hands to her black tights and got back up, still pale and clammy. "We need to find somewhere to hide."

Jen shuddered, and with a visible effort she contributed, "Anywhere we break into will have a weak point from then on. We need to get in somewhere with a key." From her pocket she pulled a clump of keys and keychains. "If we can get to my house…"

"Where's your house?" Alexis asked, already enthused by the idea.

"A few blocks that way." She pointed south.

"Unless they give up," Hazel said, nodding towards the zombies at the gate, "we'll have to leave the way we came. I think we should just break in."

"If they're blinded they won't know where we are," Jen pointed out.

"Or we could break in temporarily," Alexis suggested, "and then sneak out."

"Why not just stay then?" Hazel asked. "What's riskier, having a broken window or traveling across town?"

"It's not across town, it's only a few blocks—"

Morgan shrieked. Hazel sprang to her feet and rushed to the trampoline in time to see Morgan and Riva jumping backwards. Morgan's hands were empty and bangs sounded on the other side of the fence. One of the monsters was wielding her shovel maniacally. In the next second it came winging over the fence like a frisbee. The girls on the trampoline dropped, but Hazel had no chance. Before she could get her hands up in defence, the shovel cracked against her forehead. She saw a spark of light over her eye like two rocks striking together and felt herself fall.

Corrupted

"Haaazeeel," a voice said, both syllables elongated.

The voice was like a man and woman speaking together. The man's voice was as deep and disturbing as a demon's; the woman's as hair-raising as a witch. Hazel wrenched her eyes open. She threw the blankets off herself, eyes darting around the familiar room.

Without seeing it, Hazel knew she was in a white-stucco rancher home with a blue concrete strip at the foundation that marked the basement. She knew the front door was a simple slab of brown wood that Gran had never bothered to paint. The door was protected by a short overhang that could only shade someone if they were standing on the front steps. With the flower bushes in a line against the basement wall, other people might have found it cute. Other people couldn't see the shadow leering out the basement window.

She ran for the bedroom door and froze when she saw the shadow standing at the end of the hall. Its edges were pulsating in a way that made Hazel think her vision was blurry. Beneath its feet, the floor was torn up to reveal the bones of the house, and the basement below.

"Haaazeeeel," it said again.

"What do you want?" she screamed.

There was another scream and Hazel experienced the bizarre sensation of opening her already open eyes. She was still in bed; the bed in Gran's old guestroom.

"I thought you were still out," Jen gasped, clutching her heart.

There were footsteps thundering towards them from all over the house and Hazel cowered against the pillows.

Riva came in wielding her rake, followed by the other girls. "What? What is it?"

"Hazel woke up," Jen panted. She was laying on her stomach across the foot of the bed, a bandage covering her hip. "She was having a nightmare."

"W-why are we here?" Hazel stuttered.

"We made it to my house," Jen said. "You and I are resting. The others are blocking the place up." To the others she said, "I'll take care of her, you get back to work. At least I can do something."

Riva hesitated, but Morgan pulled her back out. Jen sat up, careful not to rip her makeshift bandage.

"How's your head?"

Hammering started up again around the house.

"Throbbing a bit," Hazel muttered.

"Do you remember what happened?"

"A zombie hit me with a shovel," she answered, her eyes still darted around the room, looking for the shadow. Kelly was standing in the corner, looking somber.

Jen grinned. "You can relax. We locked all the doors and blocked all the windows except the attic so far. The zombies only just noticed movement in here, but it's too late for them to get in."

Hazel jerked upright as embarrassment hit her. She could

picture her classmates dragging her lifeless form to safety. She could hear them groan at how heavy she was.

"I don't think they'll let you help unless we're in trouble," Jen said, misinterpreting her movement. "They wouldn't let me."

"How did you manage to get me here?" Hazel asked, attempting to sound casual.

"There was a wheelbarrow in the yard, so we used it like a wheelchair. The zombies were all blind so we let them in and snuck past them. There were a few tense moments," Jen admitted, and strain showed on her face, "but we ran."

The image of the girls struggling to get her into the wheelbarrow caused a fresh blush to crawl across Hazel's face. She wondered how many of them it had taken. She fought against embarrassment, defensiveness coming to her aid. She was worth saving and her weight had nothing to do with that. She was worth risking the other girls' lives for. She stifled the little "no" that kept resurfacing.

"We can't stay here," Hazel finally said, to nods of agreement from Kelly.

Jen's eyebrows rose in surprise. "Why not?"

Hazel opened her mouth. She made eye contact with Kelly, then finally said aloud what she had been keeping from her family her whole life. Her heart beat as fast as it did when the monsters were chasing her.

"There's something in this house. Something that killed my grandmother."

There was silence in the room apart from the pounding of the hammers.

"We don't know Gran's dead for sure," Kelly said at last, but without much conviction. "And how do you know whatever it is killed her?"

"You can tell something is here though?" Hazel said aloud.

Jen glanced into the corner where Kelly stood, then said, "No, I-I can't."

Hazel turned back to Jen. "You've lived here a few months. Didn't you feel like someone was watching you? Did you have any nightmares?"

"Well of course I did, but everyone does," she said, dismissing the idea.

"We can't stay here," Hazel repeated, getting off the bed.

"Hazel," Jen said, following her lead. "We can't leave. It's not safe out there."

"It's not safe in—"

"Look, I've lived here for months and I'm fine. I'm not even sick," Jen said, taking Hazel by the arm so that she had to meet her eye. Hazel's stomach jittered and she had to catch her breath. "We're safe from the people who want to eat us. If something in here makes us sick eventually, at least we'll be alive to deal with it. Alright?"

Hazel knew Jen was just placating her, but she thought it over nonetheless. The last time she saw the shadow had been at the hospital. Maybe it wasn't even in the house anymore. She glanced at Kelly, who was hugging herself and looking around the room.

"I guess."

Jen sat back down on the bed, one hand at her wounded hip.

"How's your...bite?" Hazel asked, thinking about contamination and how zombie TV shows dealt with it.

"It kills. But it's just punctures. You pulled that psycho off me before he could take a chunk. It's deep, but it'll heal."

Hazel drifted back towards the bed. Kelly was shaking her

head, but Hazel sat anyway. Kelly was more afraid of the supernatural than Hazel, after all. But Hazel was the one with something physical to fear if she went back outside. Little as Hazel wanted it to be, this house was their sanctuary now.

"Do you have a phone?" Hazel asked.

"Yeah," Jen said, pointing to Alexis' cellphone on the nightstand. "I left mine in the classroom. Calls don't work though," she added as Hazel seized the phone.

"Why not?"

"Well, I found an article online about shutting down service providers. It was hypothetical, but it said the government can do it in case of emergency, like a potential terrorist attack. It said it's easiest to do it in a localized area." Jen shrugged. "I think that's what's happened. You can still get on the internet though."

"So they think this is a terrorist attack?"

"Here," Jen said, and she took the phone, pulled up a news site, and handed it back to Hazel.

The headline read: *State of Emergency*. She skimmed the article.

"'Early this morning...reports of violent assaults occurring at Horizon General Hospital... Attacks have spread east across town... Victims number in the hundreds...'" She paused to digest the horror of that number.

"Keep reading," Jen said.

"'There is no clear indication as to the reason for these attacks... Citizens are encouraged to lock their doors and stay inside until further notice. On no account are these attackers to be approached... Police are investigating... Emergency response teams are attempting to restrain attackers and secure the city. Please check back for further updates as they come.'"

"And by restrain, they mean shoot," Jen said.

"What?"

"Yeah, like those ones climbing the tree. The helicopter came and shot them. They saved us."

Hazel gaped. "I had no idea."

She pictured her mother attacking her favourite patients before getting shot by some SWAT officer, with no chance at recovery. The whole image made her shiver as if with a fever. It was all wrong.

"Read the comments," Jen said.

She found a comment from someone who claimed to be a doctor and read it aloud, "'It looks to me like the victims may be experiencing a mass psychosis in which they attack others due to intense fear or posttraumatic stress. I've never heard of infecting others with aggression before, but it could be possible if the amygdala in the brain is somehow corrupted. Regardless, it seems to be very contagious... Stay far away from the corrupted, everyone. Stay safe.'"

"'Corrupted...'" Hazel repeated to herself.

Sleepover

They hunkered down in the living room together, not wanting to split up. There was a lumpy old fold-out couch, and they dragged the other two mattresses in around it. Hazel stared in shock when she first left the bedroom and saw that the girls had torn up the hardwood floor to nail over the entrances. Just like her dream, she could see down to the dark basement, where the shadow had once lurked. It was with a pounding heart that she crossed a beam to reach her grandmother's old room, but not because she was afraid of falling; the beam was thick enough. It was the possibility of a hand seizing her ankle that raised the fine hairs on her neck.

The girls had dumped the mattress in Gran's ex-room off the bed. The strips of wood from the bedframe had been too convenient to pass up. When Hazel and Alexis had slid the mattress back across the hallway beam, the room was bare apart from Jen's parents' clothes. Hazel shut the door. It seemed that Gran was gone, and she didn't want to see it.

The girls grew quiet as night came on, unable to find any news on TV. The few zombies who had noticed the banging inside the house had given up waiting for them. There was silence in the neighbourhood. Hazel had been on the verge of sending her mother an email in a pathetic attempt to contact her, when the power went out.

"What happened?" asked Riva from the kitchen, where she had been checking out the food.

Di peeked between the boards on the living room window. "I don't see anything."

Hazel glanced back down at the laptop on her knees and groaned. "Wifi's out."

"Ah," Morgan complained, shaking her phone with one hand as if it would help, "and my battery is almost dead..."

"Do you think they cut the power on purpose?" Alexis asked over her own phone.

"Seems like an evil thing to do." Morgan scowled, shutting down her phone and chucking it at the cushion next to her. "None of my texts got through either."

There was no power in the whole neighbourhood, if not the city. Kelly said she had never seen darkness like it. Jen rummaged up two flashlights and a handful of candles that made the shadows on the wall duck and dodge like people. They agreed to keep one phone running in case new information arrived, but shut off the laptop and remaining two phones to preserve the batteries.

The girls ate salad for dinner, one of the few things in the fridge that didn't need cooking. They put on Jen's family's pajamas and settled into their respective beds much earlier than normal. Hazel and Jen ended up together on a mattress on the floor. Conversation staggered along. Nothing felt appropriate for what had happened that day. Then the crying started.

"Di?" Riva whispered, sitting up in her spot on the fold-out couch.

Di was curled up on the mattress closest to the hallway.

"What is it?" Riva asked.

"Kelly..." Di squeaked, muffling her sobs with the blanket wrapped around her.

Hazel's insides stiffened. She nestled back down, pushing it all away, and found Jen's eyes on her. They listened to Riva's whispered attempts to console Di. At the edge of the room, Kelly picked her way to the foot of Di's bed, her face stricken and helpless. Hazel could hear a rushing sound in her ears.

To make matters worse, Breanna whispered, "I was going to go camping this summer with my mom and dad."

Born of past sleepovers, Hazel blurted to Jen the first diverting question that popped into her head.

"So do you like anyone?"

She cringed at her own over-correction.

Jen had the grace to smother her surprise. "No, not right now. Do you?"

Hazel blanked. She had blundered right into something she wanted to hide. "Do you like boys?" she asked instead.

Jen hesitated, then sent it right back at her, "Do you?"

"Yeah, oh yeah," Hazel gabbled over the voices across the room. "I just wondered. 'Cuz, you know, not everyone does."

"True," Jen said.

"Yeah. Sorry. I just..." she trailed off, smothering embarrassment.

"I get it," Jen said, glancing over at the inconsolable Di.

"Goodnight," Hazel said, with a weak smile to appear less abrupt.

"Goodnight."

She turned on her side and buried her ears under blankets. She fell asleep worrying that she might have just outed herself, but also that Jen might turn into a zombie and eat her in the night.

* * *

As Hazel was rolling over the next morning, she realized with a jolt that she wasn't in her own bed. She snapped her eyes open then screamed, scrambling backwards into Jen. The shadow was crouched under the fold-out couch with its face hovering in front of Hazel's.

"What? What?" Jen demanded, emerging disheveled from under the sheets.

The shadow was gone with a cackle before Hazel could point it out.

"Sorry," she gasped. "Sorry, i-it was the thing I told you about."

"What thing?"

"The thing that killed..." Hazel trailed off as Morgan groaned and sat up, followed by a few of the others.

"What's going on?"

"Nothing," Hazel said, catching her breath. "Go back to sleep."

Hazel caught Riva's eye, who shot her a questioning look.

Morgan groaned again. "I almost forgot about yesterday."

"I didn't," said Alexis, who was sleeping on the other mattress with Di. "I couldn't sleep. I kept hearing things."

"Like what?" Hazel said, too fast.

"Like footsteps and creaking. Some noises from outside. It was the worst sleep."

Hazel's rest had been terrible too, but it was a monster-filled, dead family kind of sleep, not the interrupted kind. A few of the girls grabbed phones to check if anything was working again. To calm herself, Hazel stood up and knelt on the fold-out, peering between the wood slabs of the window. She received her second jolt of the morning when she saw a pair of eyes staring back in at her. She yelped.

The zombie thrashed at the window, rattling the panes.

"Shut the curtains!" Morgan cried, scrambling out of bed.

Hazel and Riva each grabbed a curtain and yanked them shut. Glass shattered on the outside. All the girls were on their feet now, looking mismatched in Jen's family's pyjamas. They grabbed their gardening tools from beside their beds. Hazel and Morgan had switched to kitchen knives.

They hesitated a moment longer, but with the glass gone, the monster banged its fists against the bare window boards. Morgan ducked behind the curtain and they heard a squelching sound. She re-emerged with a bloody knife, looking grim.

"It didn't even faze it," she said as the banging continued.

All the girls stared at the blood on Morgan's knife.

"It's going to attract more," Morgan said, just as unfazed. "If they don't feel pain anymore, we'll have to start killing them. In the movies it's always a head shot, right?"

Hazel gave her head a little shake and leaned over the back of the couch next to Morgan. "It won't work. I smashed in a girl's head in the auto shop yesterday and she just kept on going."

She had not yet stabbed one of the monsters. It was too much like stabbing a human in the eye for comfort, but after being wheeled all the way to Jen's house, she needed to carry her weight. She masked her face and raised the knife in her fist. Another monster joined the first, thrashing at the window. She took her aim through the gap between board and windowpane as Morgan blinded her target.

"Here...thingy-thingy-thingy?" Hazel called to the other.

Its eye appeared at the gap. She thrust the knife in, more

startled than prepared. There was a sickening pop, and the knife slid forward so that Hazel fell into the boards, having expected more resistance. Morgan pulled her back up. The knife dropped to the ground as the zombie yanked away from the window. Next second, its other eye appeared. Morgan's knife flashed up and stabbed.

There was a roar of frustration from the other side, but not pain. Hazel and Morgan shared the gap as they watched the zombies continue to bang against the house. The eyes were pouring blood, but they remained open. One strained its neck and jerked its head side-to-side, but it still couldn't see. Then it stumbled in the garden and went down. When it stood up it was just past the window and before the stairs. The sound of thuds against the side of the house weren't quite as bad.

Hazel turned around to see all the girls watching her, including Kelly and Breanna. She couldn't gauge if she had impressed or disturbed them.

Pull your Weight

"Any others out there?" Alexis asked.

Hazel scanned the street. "There's lots."

"There's a couple," Morgan countered. "They're coming this way. We need more boards over this window."

Without breakfast, the girls got to work. Riva had the idea to take down the gyprock from the inner kitchen wall and cover the boarded front window with a huge slab. They needed an X-ACTO knife and a drill, but Jen said they had both in the basement. Before Hazel could stop them, Alexis and Di headed towards the stairs, which were behind a door off the kitchen.

"Kelly," Hazel said aloud, terrified the shadow would attack them.

"I'll watch out for them," Kelly reassured her, and she darted to the stairs before the other two.

"What's down there?" Breanna asked.

"What about Kelly?" Jen asked at the same time. Her tone suggested she was afraid of snapping Hazel in two.

"Nothing," Hazel lied. "I was just thinking out loud."

Morgan, Riva, and Jen all exchanged a look. Hazel realized she could get away with a lot of crazy behaviour with a dead sister. Riva sidestepped the moment by handing Hazel a hammer that was still left out from yesterday. With her ears on alert, Hazel headed to her old bedroom to take apart the bedframe. To her relief, Alexis and Di returned with the tools they needed a minute later. Kelly looked like she had just seen a horror movie.

"What is it?" Hazel asked when they were alone in the bedroom and Riva had started slicing away at the kitchen wall. Hazel bent over the bedframe in case anyone walked in.

"I saw it," Kelly said with a shudder. "The thing that was killing Gran."

Hazel's eyes widened. She felt an unexpected warmth in her chest and it took a moment to realize she was feeling relieved. It was so good not to be the only one. Her eyes prickled. Breanna, having followed the only two people she could communicate with, stared between the sisters.

"It was just standing in the middle of the room," Kelly whimpered, "staring at me like it was happy I could see it."

"But it didn't do anything?"

Kelly shook her head.

Hazel sighed and wrenched a nail out of the bedframe. "It must feel powerful, scaring us without doing anything... But why isn't it doing anything? And why is it back here?"

"Why didn't you ever tell me?" Kelly asked.

Hazel swallowed. "I was afraid you wouldn't..." she trailed off and changed her answer, "I didn't want to scare you."

"But it was real!" Kelly said, cheeks reddening with anger. "It was killing Gran and you didn't say anything!"

Hazel's face burned at the accusation. "I didn't know for sure until I saw it with her at the hospital."

"Still—"

"What could anyone have done if I told them?"

Breanna shifted and mumbled, "Should I go?"

"What about that stuff you use around the house?" Kelly demanded, ignoring her.

"What stuff?"

"The stuff you burn that Mom thought you were smoking."

"You know about that?" Hazel asked, mouth gaping.

"Well, yeah. You've been doing it for years, you think no one noticed?"

Hazel recovered her composure. "Lavender is for ghosts. I don't know if it would work on...it. And I couldn't have gotten into Gran's house and smoked it up without anyone noticing."

"You should have figured it out!" Kelly snapped. "Was keeping your secret really more important than saving Gran's life?"

Hazel hacked at the bedframe with a hollow ache in her chest and shame burning in her gut. Kelly was saying the worst words her inner voice had ever spewed.

"You thought it was hard before," Kelly said to her back, "now you have to cross a town full of zombies."

"What?" Hazel turned back in spite of herself.

"To get the lavender! If you don't try, it'll kill one of you next."

Hazel adjusted her squat so she was leaning more on her right leg. Her heels still ached from jumping out of the French room window. "Not for years."

"You think," Kelly corrected.

"Yeah, I do. But I'll be killed instantly if I leave," Hazel said. "And for something that might not even work."

"It's that or convince the others to find a different hiding place. If this goes on long enough you'll need more food anyway. Maybe you don't have to go all the way home for the stuff. Where do you get it?"

"That little hippie store in the plaza."

Apart from a corner store, Hazel and Kelly lived in a neighbourhood without shops. The L-shaped plaza was the nearest thing, boasting a dollar store, pharmacy, restaurant, barber shop, flower shop, and the new age store. The store was called Natural Life, and it was about four kilometres away from Jen's. Home was a little closer, but it was also nearer to the school and the influx of monsters.

"That's a long walk," Breanna said. "I used to work at the dollar store and I always got a ride."

Kelly's face screwed up in frustration. "You could find a car."

"And hot-wire it? I don't know how!" Hazel said.

"Look it up!"

"How am I supposed to hide that from the others when we're watching our battery use?"

"Arrghhh!" Kelly roared, throwing up her hands. "Stop making excuses!"

"It's not excuses, it's logic!"

There was a crash above them that shook the house. All three girls stared at the ceiling, petrified.

"What was that?" someone called from the kitchen as all the hammering paused.

The ceiling creaked. Kelly, Hazel, and Breanna followed the noise out to the living room. Riva, Alexis, Morgan, Di, and Jen's eyes were all glued to the ceiling.

"I think one got in," Riva whispered.

"Can it get down?" Alexis asked through her own fingernails.

"There's an opening in the bedroom closet," Jen said. "It's just a slab."

"Can we block it somehow?"

"We could do what we're doing for the living room, but the

hammering will attract it."

"We should have taken out its ears, and its eyes," Morgan said.

"Might not be the same one," Hazel said. "There had to be at least forty out there, that I could see."

Morgan frowned and opened her mouth to speak, but there was another crash from above.

"Another one," Di said, going paler than ever. "They're climbing the house."

"Let's go," Morgan said, and she shoved a hammer into the waistband of her pants, grabbed two fistfuls of the nails, and dashed off to the bedroom.

Hazel was right behind her, tackling the dismembering of the bedframe with added fervour. Di took the wood from her and handed it to Morgan in the closet, in an assembly line. There was a splintering sound from the living room.

"No!" came Alexis' shriek.

The girls almost pushed each other over in their race to get back to the living room, tripping over the mattress. Alexis had lunged across the couch and was struggling to keep a long board in place at the window. A huge zombie was pushing back. Hazel saw the scene in the French room again, when Alexis had kept the monsters at bay by guarding the door. Adrenaline tingled in her toes. Breanna had died when the door opened.

One end of the board had come loose and the nails wouldn't slip back into the window frame. The monster fought an arm through and clawed Alexis' left arm. Blood spurted and oozed down her forearm in deep scratches. Riva rushed to her rescue, but the monster stopped tugging at the boards and tried to pull Alexis out the window instead. It seized her bleeding arm by the elbow and yanked her forward so that she cut her lip against the wood. Her scream was so shrill it was like a stab to the eardrums.

Before Hazel could move, there was another jarring sound. It was like the hiccoughing-laugh of an infant. In the door of the basement stood the shadow, its mouth agape in a grin that showed an even deeper black down its throat.

Riva grabbed Alexis around the waist and yanked her back so that they both toppled over the end of the mattress. Jen nudged Hazel aside, and when she looked back at the shadow, it had gone. Jen rammed a hammer against the board and the nails found a new home in the wall. She pounded away at it until it was secure again.

"Get me that gyprock!" she yelled.

Morgan pushed past Hazel and Di to take over Riva's hack-job at the kitchen wall.

"You two, get back to work on the attic!" she ordered over her shoulder.

Hazel responded to the order without thinking. In the bedroom, she grabbed a loose chunk of the bed and thrust it up at the roof of the closet. She needed a chair if she was going to reach.

Alexis' blood had spattered her arm, and when she sensed Kelly enter the room behind her, she ignored Di and asked, "Is it bad? Is Alexis okay?"

Di answered, but Hazel didn't hear her as Kelly said, "It bit the meaty part of her arm, so I don't think it hit an artery. But she needs stitches."

"What am I doing?" Hazel cried, and she dropped the wood again. "Kelly, tell me what to do!"

She raced out of the room, leaving Di looking bewildered and tiny with a chunk of bedframe in her arms. Hazel crossed the fold-out and dropped to her knees at Alexis' side. Riva was tightening a strip of blanket around the bloody elbow. The white sheet was already red.

"Hazel, get back in there!" Morgan said.

"She needs stitches," Hazel said to Riva, ignoring her. "Trade spots with me."

"You got this?" Riva asked, surprised.

Hazel nodded. "Di needs your help with the attic."

"We need a sewing needle, thread, and alcohol," Kelly said. "Or a lighter."

Riva left her to it. Hazel repeated Kelly's instructions to Jen, who was swinging her hammer at the fingers that kept slashing through the gaps in the window.

"Jen!" she yelled.

"There's sewing stuff in my parents' closet," Jen said.

"So go get it!" Hazel said. "They don't feel pain anymore, you're wasting your time!"

"Oh," Jen said, pausing. "Right."

She let the hammer bounce onto the mattress and ran off to the master bedroom. She and Di danced around each other in the hallway as Di came to retrieve a kitchen chair.

"Ok, now what?" Hazel asked.

"Alcohol to clean it," Kelly said.

"We need alcohol to clean it," she repeated to Jen. "Check the bathroom cabinet?"

Alexis whimpered.

"It's not too bad, Alexis," Hazel told her. "We'll get it cleaned up and everything, don't worry."

Alexis shook her head and whispered, "I s-saw things."

"Outside?"

"No, i-in my head."

"What do you mean?"

"When it grabbed me, I knew it was biting me and where I was, but I could see my...my brother." Her voice squeaked at the word. "He was trapped at home in the closet and they were ripping him apart and he was screaming for me to help him, but I couldn't! He's only nine, Hazel! He's only nine..." She burst into tears.

"It wasn't real," Hazel said, grabbing Alexis' shoulders in an attempt to sooth her. "He's probably fine."

Alexis' despairing sob spoke on her behalf.

"Where was he yesterday when everything happened?"

"At school," came the choked reply.

The elementary school was a few blocks to the north of the high school.

"The zombies—"

Alexis cringed at the word. "The corrupt," she corrected, using the word from the news story Jen had found.

"Right. As far as we know, his school went into lockdown before anything could happen. He's probably still there now."

"You think so?" Alexis asked, pulling back to look into Hazel's face.

"Yeah, he's probably giddy he got to have a sleepover at school with all his friends."

Alexis smiled in spite of herself, but the worry never left her brow.

"I don't think he could be in a safer place," Hazel continued as Jen arrived with the sewing kit and rubbing alcohol. "All those teachers, the medical supplies, the packed lunches and extra food for the kids who don't have anything. They have those metal shutters for the windows. I wish we had been there."

"But it looked real," Alexis whispered.

"Mine did too," Jen said, passing Hazel the sewing kit. "It was the scariest thing I've ever seen."

Hazel paused with her hands out to receive the supplies.

"Me too," said Kelly and Breanna.

Jen avoided their eyes as she went on, "When the one at school bit me, I saw myself getting pushed off this huge cliff. I was so high there was no way I could survive, and there were rocks and giant waves at the bottom. But the fall went on forever. I felt like I was losing my mind and there was nothing I could do." Reliving the experience made her breathless. She took a big, shaking one now and said, "I kept dreaming about it last night."

There was silence.

"Stop sitting around!" Morgan yelled at them.

They all jumped.

Jen joined Morgan, who was getting ready to carry the huge slab of gyprock over to the window. Alexis and Hazel retreated to the kitchen to get out of the way. Kelly and Breanna tagged along.

"Sit here," Hazel said, indicating one of the few chairs they hadn't broken down for scraps.

She looked to Kelly for advice as she poured alcohol on a cloth and dabbed at the wound and scratches. Alexis scrunched up her face, but didn't speak. Hazel soaked the needle and thread in alcohol for sterilization as well, then hesitated, needle in hand.

"I never wanted to be a nurse," she admitted.

"You never wanted to stab anyone in the eye, either, and that was grosser than this," Kelly replied.

Hazel smirked, then set to work, following Kelly's instructions.

"How do you know how to do this?" Alexis asked, staring at the magnets on the fridge as a distraction.

"My sister," Hazel said. "She wants to be a doctor."

Kelly paused in her instructions and Hazel regretted using the present tense. She encouraged Kelly past it. "Come on, let's do this."

She dug the needle under a flap of skin and Alexis tensed. Hazel gritted her teeth. She pushed the needle into the other flap, pulled it through, and tugged the skin together. She tied a knot, then started again. It was far worse than stabbing an attacking monster in the eye. Alexis didn't say a word, but her cringes caused Hazel pain. Breanna had to walk away.

"Ah, I hate this," she said through clenched teeth as the digging and tensing went on and on.

"I'm sorry," Alexis breathed.

"It's not you. I hate hurting you."

"You're helping me," she corrected.

The bite wound was a jagged half-moon and proved more difficult to seal than the scratches. She had to cut off excess skin with kitchen scissors to make a smooth base for the needle. In the end there were nine stitches there and five or six down each scratch. When they were finished, all three girls let out a sigh of relief. Hazel wrapped up Alexis' entire forearm and was glad she didn't have to look at it anymore.

"I'm glad we have you, Hazel," Alexis said.

She pulled Hazel into a one-armed hug. Surprised but gratified, Hazel hugged her back. When she pulled away, she saw Kelly beaming at her with pride.

Training

Whenever Alexis closed her eyes, she saw the monsters ripping her brother apart; whenever Jen closed her eyes she saw herself being pushed off a cliff; whenever Hazel closed her eyes, she saw the shadow giggling about Alexis' close call. Di cried every night, grieving over Kelly, while Kelly wept beside her. Riva and Morgan were the only ones who appeared to be holding it together. But with the banging around upstairs, no one was getting a solid sleep.

As an added bonus, every time Hazel opened her eyes the shadow was looming over her. She hated going to sleep at night. She tried taking frequent naps instead, but it only gave the shadow extra opportunities to send a jolt down to Hazel's fingertips and toes. Each time she wondered if the shadow was moving in for the kill, but then it was gone, content, for the moment, with torture. The other girls thought she was suffering from post-traumatic stress. Riva was there to help calm her down.

"It's okay, you're safe," she would whisper, putting a sooth-ing arm around Hazel, even in the dead of night.

"We're not safe," Hazel would reply, noticing Jen avoiding eye contact. She would hold Riva's other hand in hers until her breathing slowed.

Riva was the oldest in her family. The twins were brother and sister toddlers with the same angular eyebrows as Riva, and eyes that disappeared when they smiled. Hazel sometimes felt like a toddler when Riva came to her side, but she had a suspicion that Riva took comfort in her role. Their friendship used to be loud, by accident: the only black girl in the school and the fat girl, best friends. Now there was a quiet solidarity in it. They had always protected each other from the odd bully their bodies attracted. The promise of protection was perhaps the one thing that had not changed.

"Where do you think they are?" she asked Riva one morning, a few days into the outbreak.

"I think the twins are probably still at the preschool." She paused, guilt crossing her face. "I was supposed to pick them up... But the church the preschool's in is mostly made of stone."

Hazel nodded. She wanted to believe they were safe too. She listened to the thrumming sound of another helicopter flying over the house.

"And Mom and Dad, I don't know," Riva went on. "They might be together. They don't work far apart."

She noticed Hazel's preoccupation. Riva reached over and squeezed her shoulder. They didn't speak about Hazel's family.

"At least we don't have to write exams," Riva sighed.

"Or buy prom dresses," Hazel added. She had been struggling to find a dress the right size, and was getting desperate as the date approached.

Jen and Morgan both groaned, overhearing. They had obviously wasted their money.

Morgan almost never mentioned her life or family. At school she had the largest friend group of all the girls, but in Jen's house she chopped vegetables alone in the kitchen, she read a book in a crack of sunlight, and she listened to the girls' talk without commenting. Hazel had Riva, and Di and Alexis were growing close over the loss of their respective friends, Kelly and Breanna. Jen blended the groups together with easy conversation. But even Jen couldn't drag Morgan out of her gloomy solitude.

"There's no point wondering where my mom and dad are," Morgan said when Jen pressed her as everyone shared lunch, "I'll find out when I find out."

Yet as soon as there was a job to be done, Morgan came to life. She handed out roles like she was in charge. Hazel caught Alexis and Di, the two grade elevens, exchanging an annoyed look when Morgan told them what chores to do. Hazel wasn't the only one who didn't enjoy being told what to do without discussion.

The first few days of hiding had been spent on fortifying and reinforcing what the corrupt tore down. It was easy to hide from grief and fear when they kept themselves busy, but then the work slowed down. They got tired of the circular conversations about when rescue would come. The girls resorted to searching the house for entertainment. So far they had found books to read, journals to steal pages from, a couple of board games, puzzles, and a deck of cards. It was not easy to use any of these in the dark, but some summer sunshine did seep in during the day, so they took advantage of their distractions while they could.

By the fourth day of hiding, Jen was pacing.

Riva set down the cards she was shuffling. "Jen, I'm sorry, but you're driving me crazy."

"I miss basketball," Jen said, flopping onto the fold-out instead.

"I miss wrestling," Hazel agreed. Just last night she had been worrying about Coach Tom.

"Oh," Alexis said, stuffing a bookmark into the novel she was reading, "speaking of wrestling...."

"Yeah?" Hazel asked.

"I was wondering if you'd give us some tips. In case we need them against the corrupt."

"Oh," Hazel said. "Yeah, okay! Sure!"

She was already on her feet. The other girls perked up with interest. Hazel pulled a mattress into the centre of the living room. Riva and Jen helped her put away the fold-out for more space.

"Can I go first?" Jen asked. She positioned herself across from Hazel, crouching low like Hazel was her check in basketball.

Hazel smiled as her heart fluttered. "That's a good stance. One foot in front with more weight on that foot. Both feet a little wider than your shoulders. Now crouch so you have a lower centre of gravity. But don't stretch your arms out. Keep your elbows in and hands out in front of you."

The girls adjusted themselves around the room to try it.

"Okay," Hazel said. "Good. But let's do an escape first. It might help against the corrupt. So say Jen is corrupt and she chased me until I fell."

Jen moved behind her and Hazel got down on her hands and knees to illustrate. "So Jen will grab me around my waist. I'm going to move my foot, whichever one I can, away from her and try to plant it."

Jen didn't do the job halfway. She grabbed Hazel in a tight embrace. Hazel felt a thrill of excitement. Competition and respect flooded her body. She forgot all about going slow so the girls could see the move, and swept her foot to the side. She planted it and pushed her back against Jen until she was standing back up. At the same time she grabbed Jen's right wrist from around her waist and pulled forward so Jen was off balance. Pivoting to the left, she dragged Jen's hand down until Jen collapsed onto her back on the mattress.

"Whoo!" Jen cheered. She bounced back up, delight all over her face. "That was fun! My turn!"

They swapped. Hazel knew it wasn't fair, but she pulled out her counter moves so Jen couldn't take her down. Jen grinned and attacked from the front. Hazel parried, and next second, Jen was on the mattress again. After a few more attempts, they were both sweating and clutching their stomachs from laughter.

"Okay, I have no idea what's going on," Riva said, shaking her head and chuckling. "You guys have to slow down."

"Yeah, I probably shouldn't have done that," Jen agreed. "My bite feels like it opened a bit."

"Oh, sorry, you're right," Hazel said, as Jen checked on the wound.

Some small drops of blood were seeping from the scabs. Despite that, it was healing quite well, and Jen still showed no signs of turning into a zombie. It appeared contamination did not spark the transformation. Hazel suspected the terror-visions paired with a fatal attack were what did the trick.

"Come here, then, Riva," Hazel said.

She demonstrated the escape with Riva, then the others. They spent a few hours practicing without interruption from either zombie or shadow. Hazel never wanted to stop.

"Yes!" Alexis called from the living room.

"What?" came five voices.

Everyone joined her from various parts of the house. Di

arrived from changing in the bedroom. She wore the same clothes as the first day, the baggy beige-knit cardigan, white t-shirt, and jean shorts. They had been hanging up to dry in the bathroom for a few days as the girls had had to hand-wash their clothes. Alexis was sitting on the fold-out mattress with the last working cellphone in her hands. Each day the girls stacked the two bedroom mattresses against the walls so they would have more walking room, but they never bothered with the fold-out.

"I haven't been sleeping very well so whenever I wake up I check to see if anyone has responded," Alexis began.

"You shouldn't do that," Di said. "The light won't help you sleep. And you'll kill the battery."

"The dark isn't exactly helping either," Alexis countered, impatient with excitement.

It was true. Within the week, they had all grown sick of the constant darkness.

"Anyway, I only look for a couple seconds. But we finally got something!"

The girls' responses overlapped.

"We did?"

"Who was it?"

"What did they say?"

"I have no idea who," Alexis said, pointing to the unknown number, "but it's about one of those texts we sent our families with all of our names and Jen's address. It says: 'Your names and address have been added to our records. Stay inside until further notice.'"

They all stood with their mouths open for a second, then Riva shrieked, "Alexis, you genius!"

Morgan punched her arm in celebration while Di did a happy

jig. Hazel grinned as Jen hugged Alexis over the laptop.

Alexis smiled and blushed. "We all sent the message. I just happened to read it."

"It was your idea!" Riva reminded her. "You might have just saved us!"

Before they knew it, they were all dancing around and punching the air while Alexis swayed in a triumphant half-dance on the bed. Kelly and Breanna spun circles around them, neither one noticing that their feet left the ground. Their corrupt friends upstairs were riled up by the noise and started pacing.

When they had all collapsed onto the bed, feet dangling, Riva said to the ceiling, "Thank goodness. The food is getting low. I was starting to worry about doing a grocery run."

"I was worrying that I'd have to start eating meat," Di said. She had been surviving on grains with the odd helping of rationed fruit and vegetables.

Hazel sat up. The shadow was crawling upside-down on the ceiling, hissing. She channelled her fright into anger and gave it the middle finger.

Jen saw and laughed. "Yeah, screw you, zombies!"

The girls all raised their middle fingers. Hazel threw the shadow a grin. It fixed her with a menacing glare and snapped its jaws before vanishing. So far all the shadow had done was torment her, but that didn't mean it wasn't capable of worse. She brushed away the worry that she would pay for that later. She hadn't yet, after all.

Hooks

"So what should we do today?" Riva asked.

"I have too much energy," Jen said, flopping her limbs around on the bed like a child. "I need to move. I wish we had music."

"I have my iPod," Riva said. "I broke the screen jumping out of the French room window, but it works." She went rummaging through her small collection of possessions. "You got speakers somewhere?"

Jen grinned and dashed off to her room to dig up a set of tiny, battery-powered speakers. "We'll probably get a few hours out of these!"

"Not too loud," Morgan said.

Hazel just restrained herself from a sarcastic retort. Nevertheless, she went to the door to see how many of the corrupt they were dealing with today. They had drilled a hole through the kitchen table and nailed it over the front door. This way, Hazel was able to look through the peephole. She could see what she guessed were about sixty corrupt wandering around.

"There's like sixty out there today," she said.

"What?" Morgan gasped. She rushed over to join Hazel and took a turn at the door. "No there isn't!"

Hazel looked again. "Yeah there is, they're all over the place.

You shouldn't be surprised, they must have corrupted more people since the beginning."

"Yeah, of course there are more. But I see maybe half that! Where are you looking?"

One of the people out there gestured for her to come outside. Hazel's mouth fell open. Then two and two added up. There were no blood stains on the man, and Morgan couldn't see him. He was a ghost, and so were half the people out there.

"Never mind, I guess I overestimated."

"Don't scare us like that," Di said with a sigh, clutching at her sweater.

Hazel gave Kelly and Breanna a meaningful look. Di glanced over her shoulder to see what Hazel was looking at. Hazel excused herself to go to the bathroom. The two ghosts followed.

When she had shut the door, she said, "There's a ghost out there waving at me."

Both of their eyebrows shot up.

"How did it see you?" Kelly frowned. "They can't see through doors."

Hazel frowned. "It wanted someone in here to come outside," she said, folding her arms as she sat on the edge of the bathtub. "Could only be me, right?"

"I'll check it out," Kelly said.

Breanna hesitated, took a deep breath, and said, "I'll come with you. But how do we get out?"

It was Hazel's turn to raise her eyebrows. "Walk through the walls?"

Both ghosts exchanged a look.

"What?" Hazel asked.

"We haven't tried it before," Breanna said. She fiddled with the zipper on her lavender sweater.

Before Hazel could say anything else, Kelly sighed in resignation and said, "Come on, let's go."

They left through the closed bathroom door. When they were gone, Hazel thought about what it meant for the two girls to pass through the walls by choice. They had to accept that they were dead. She stared at her toes, regretting having pushed them. But she hadn't failed to notice how brave Kelly was being these days. She had gone into the basement to watch over her friends, now she was going outside with all the corrupt. Maybe she really was accepting her death. Nothing could hurt her now.

Then again, they didn't know what the shadow could do to her, or where she would go if she moved on. Then there was the fact that she was still hanging around the living. The dead were not supposed to stick around. They always tried to interfere in the lives of the living if they had a medium to work through. Hazel's research informed her that people started asking mediums in hiding questions, like, "How did you know that?" and, "Have you been going through my stuff?" But for the dead it was heartbreaking to be left out of the world.

Hazel had never tested this theory, but she didn't want that fate for Kelly. Kelly would have to move on, no matter how scary it might be. Hazel rubbed her eyes. She had helped countless ghosts move on, but never anyone she couldn't bare to part with. It was going to be so much harder, but eventually she would have to do what no one else could. She would have to be Kelly's guide.

She stood up to check how teary her eyes were in the mirror and gasped so shrill it was almost a scream. The shadow was grinning at her from the bathtub. All around it stood bleeding people, filling the tub, standing in their own blood. They faded into the wall behind, like there were too many to fit. She spun around, clutching the counter for support. She couldn't see the people, but to her alarm, the shadow was still standing there amidst the shampoo bottles and razors.

"Who are you?" she asked the people who had vanished, her brain struggling to catch up with her beating heart.

There was no answer, and when Hazel glanced back at the mirror, they weren't there either. She turned back to the shadow, who had advanced on her, making her jump.

"Stop doing that!" she shouted into its face. "Get away from me!"

It lifted its chin and seemed to breathe in her scent through its mouth. There was a sound like distant screams coming from its gullet.

"What do you want?" she screamed.

In that same, deep male voice paired with the chilling female one it whispered, "More life..."

Then it was gone. Hazel collapsed onto the toilet, her knees weak. There was a knock at the bathroom door.

"Hazel? Hazel, are you okay?" came Riva's voice.

"I'm fine," she squeaked.

"Why were you yelling?"

"I–I was...grieving?" she lied, playing the dead sister card again. She cringed at the pathetic lie. Her brain didn't seem to be working.

There was a pause on the other side of the door. "May I come in?"

Hazel gulped a huge breath to steady herself. "It's open."

Riva entered. The expression on her face was so miserable and sympathetic that Hazel felt her eyes tear up again. Riva didn't say anything. She knelt at the toilet and pulled Hazel into a fierce embrace. Hazel fought to stop herself from trembling.

"I wish there was something I could do," Riva sniffed, and Hazel realized she was crying.

She pulled back. "There's nothing anyone can do. That's why it's so frustrating."

Outside, the music came on. It was an upbeat pop song, decades old.

"Come on," Riva said, standing up and wiping at her eyes. "We can forget for a minute."

"Just give me another second," Hazel said, pretending to fix the makeup she had borrowed from Jen in the mirror. "I'll be right out."

Riva left, and Breanna and Kelly returned.

"So?" she asked the ghosts, trying to act normal.

The girls looked unnerved. "The guy was telling us to get out of here. He said we'll all be killed."

"He said it has its hooks in us," Breanna said. "And if we look we can see them."

"What does that mean?" Hazel frowned, eyes still darting to the empty tub.

"He means the thing that lives here."

"He knows about the shadow?"

The two ghosts exchanged another look.

"What?"

"The hooks," they said together.

"The guy had one," Kelly went on, hugging herself. "And it led straight into the house."

"What do you mean hooks?"

"It's a connection. Close your eyes."

Hazel did as she was told.

"Now feel for the connections you have to other people. Try Riva." Kelly waited so Hazel could try. "You automatically feel a cord heading out to where she is, right?"

Eyes still shut, Hazel's eyebrows raised. That was exactly what she felt.

"And one to me."

Hazel nodded. That one was easy to find.

"Open your eyes."

Hazel opened her eyes. For a moment she could see a blue cord connecting her heart to Kelly's, but it faded away like a trick of the light.

"But there's another one," Kelly went on, and Hazel didn't like her darker tone. "Try it again."

Hazel shut her eyes and tried to feel for this mysterious "other one." With a sinking feeling, she located a tight sensation in her back, like a hook tugging at her. She imagined a dark cord, like an ugly steel cable, and followed it down into the basement. There she lost her nerve and snapped her eyes back open.

Kelly nodded, looking frightened. "See?"

"Why are we connected to it?" Hazel asked, panicked.

"It wants us," Breanna said, and her glum face went pale.

"It had something to do with our deaths," said Kelly. "The ghosts are all afraid of it."

The pop music bounced on.

The Truth

"Hazel, come on!" Alexis called from the living room, out of breath from dancing.

"We just got word out that we're here," Hazel said to Kelly and Breanna, referring to the message Alexis had sent. "If we just hang in there a little longer, we'll get out of here before it can—"

"That guy out there was never in here," Kelly argued. "This thing has a really long reach."

"Well, what do we do then?"

"You need to try the lavender."

Hazel gave a sigh of despair.

"It might work!"

"There's a lot of risk involved in that 'might!'"

"According to this guy, that hook will go with you wherever you go. Rescue won't matter. You have to do something."

"I think the girls would notice if I started taking down boards and then took off."

"You can't go alone," Kelly agreed. "You have to tell them."

Hazel's chest constricted. "They wouldn't believe me!"

"You'll have to convince them!"

Hazel stared at the two ghosts with her mouth open, shaking her head in disbelief.

"Use us," Breanna said. "We can tell you stuff about the others you shouldn't know. They'll have to believe we're still here."

"I don't know..."

The ghosts didn't seem to realize the lavender would chase them away as well. Hazel didn't know how to break it to them. Just then the other girls danced past the bathroom in a synchronized line. A slow smile crept up on Hazel's face. The second they were out of sight, she could hear them giggling like children. Hazel, Breanna, and Kelly couldn't help but roll their eyes and grin.

That evening, as the sun went down, Kelly and Breanna hissed things in Hazel's ear that she should tell the others. They kept up such a consistent stream that Hazel wanted to cover her ears.

"You've been quiet today," Di commented from where she lay across the fold-out. She settled her chin on her arms and looked down at Hazel on the mattress below.

Kelly shot her a 'now' look.

"I've been thinking," Hazel replied, still reluctant.

"About what?" Di asked, as some of the other girls tuned in.

Hazel took a deep breath, her heart slamming around in her chest. "Did Jen tell you that this place is haunted?"

In the candlelight, Di's crinkled forehead had deep shadows. "Haunted?"

"Yeah," Hazel nodded. "I found out when I was a kid and my Gran lived here."

"That's a terrible joke," came Morgan's unimpressed voice.

"It's just a creepy house," Jen said.

Hazel focused on Di. "Have you noticed anything?"

"No... I mean, sometimes I feel like someone is behind me.

But that's paranoia. We...we've been through a lot."

Hazel shook her head and fiddled with the blankets. "It's more than that."

"Hazel..." Riva's gentle tone urged her to stop.

"Kelly says," Hazel continued, taking another steadying breath, "that you failed your driver's test."

There was silence.

"She told you that?" Di asked, and her voice was shocked and hurt. "That was supposed to be a secret. It's... I'm so embarrassed..."

"She also told me," Hazel went on, "that you became a vegetarian to spite your uncle. But then you realized it was wrong to eat animals when you had enough vegetables to eat. So you stuck with it."

"What does this have to do with anything?" Di squeaked.

"She told me this today."

The silence was profound. Even the zombies upstairs seemed to have stopped moving.

"This isn't about my sanity," Hazel mumbled. "I've always been able to see ghosts. And I have more."

She went on, listing poor Di's fears and secrets. She even threw out that Breanna knew Alexis had once slapped her own father. After a while, both Di and Alexis got angry.

"How do you really know this?" Alexis demanded.

"They're standing right beside me," Hazel said. "Didn't you wonder why I wasn't more upset about Kelly? But I'm telling you this for a reason. Listen: there's a shadow in this house, and it killed my Gran, and it will kill us too if we don't get rid of it. Kelly wants me to burn lavender, she thinks it might work. I used to do it to keep the ghosts out of our house. She thinks I should try using it to chase away the shadow. But to get it I either have to go home or go to the plaza."

Here she paused to take in the shocked expressions on the faces around her. Breanna was their classmate who they never thought they would see again, which was alarming enough. But Kelly was her sister. That made Hazel seem plain crazy.

Before anyone could suggest Hazel was having a mental breakdown, the bathroom door handle rattled. Everyone turned to stare at it. There was no mistaking the way it turned all the way around. The door opened without a creak. No one visible was on the other side.

"I've never seen that happen before," Jen said, and Hazel could tell it made her uneasy.

"It's just a door," Morgan said, after yet another silent moment.

On the opposite side of them, the basement door slammed. Di and Alexis both shrieked. Everyone with feet on the floor drew them up like there was a spider running around. Hazel tried to suppress a thrumming in her ears. The shadow had never exposed itself to another living person before. Hazel had never thought it possible. Was it so angry she had shared the secret of its existence? Or was it trying to chase them out, to their deaths among the corrupt?

"So there's a breeze," Morgan scoffed, setting her feet back down as if convincing herself she wasn't scared. "We should make sure it's not big enough for a zombie to break through."

She got up and went into the bathroom, everyone else holding their breath. In another minute she came back out, her face placid and unconcerned.

"It probably came from the vent."

"And turned the door handle?" Di asked in a small voice.

Morgan shrugged. Then there was laughter from the basement. Morgan backed into the standing mattress in shock and it fell to the floor.

"Shhh!" Riva hissed at her.

"Can you all hear that?" Hazel whispered.

There was a collective nod.

"Who's down there?" Morgan whispered. "And how did they get in?"

"It's the shadow," Hazel said. "It's been here the whole time. We locked ourselves in with it."

Di clapped a hand over her mouth.

"Stop freaking everyone out, Hazel!" Morgan said, throwing her a disgusted look.

"It's not me, it's it! It's been terrorizing me since I was six."

Riva stood up and went to the basement door.

"Riva, don't!" Alexis said.

"Hello?" Riva called down the stairs. "Who's down there?"

"Nightmares," came the double-voiced reply.

Kelly and Di both squealed and the living and dead friends squeezed together on the fold-out without realizing it.

"You're all going to die," the voice gloated.

"Riva, shut the door!" Jen croaked.

"Nightmares and death," the voice said, growing louder. "Nightmares and death!"

Riva moved to slam the basement door shut, but a black hand reached out of the darkness and grabbed her wrist. Everyone in the house screamed. Riva jerked her wrist back so hard she fell. She scrambled backwards, kicking the door shut with her foot before stumbling into the living room. Everyone was on their feet. Morgan and Jen snatched up gardening weapons.

"Block the door!" Morgan cried.

"It's not a zombie!" Hazel said. "The door doesn't matter!"

"Grab your weapons," Riva said, her entire body shaking. "We have to go, now."

"Won't it follow us?" Alexis asked as she fished for her shears.

They looked to Hazel.

"I don't know."

Morgan was sliding debris towards the basement door. "We can't leave!"

"Lavender, you said?" Riva asked, ignoring her.

Hazel nodded.

Di was wringing her hands. "Front door or back door?"

"Front is farther from...it," Riva replied.

"We can take on one person in here better than a bunch of the corrupt out there!" Morgan said.

"We can't take on something that's not a person," Hazel countered.

She scooped up the remaining weapons and shoved them into the girls' hands. Then she grabbed the drill, put it in reverse, and started taking the nails out of the kitchen table that blocked the front door. Jen stood at her back, gripping the gardening hoe like a baseball bat and staring at the basement.

"Are you crazy?" Morgan cried. She tried to wrestle the drill out of Hazel's hands.

"Morgan, stop!" Hazel said through clenched teeth, struggling to keep ahold of the drill.

Riva seized Morgan around the waist and dragged her away. Morgan grabbed the couch to resist.

"Look at my wrist, Morgan!" Riva cried.

She shoved her arm into Morgan's face. There were red welts in the shape of fingers—if those fingers had been burning hot.

"People can't do that." She threw a glance over her shoulder at the basement door. "Get us out of here, Hazel."

Hazel finished with the table, Morgan looking torn. The other girls helped her move it aside. Peering through the peephole, Hazel was careful to count only those who were bloody. Her eyes paused on a man's body lying face-down on the grass. In the twilight, she could see a dark pool around him. He didn't fit either the corrupt or the ghost category.

"I see about thirty," Hazel said, tearing her gaze away from him. "Some of them are heading this way with all that screaming we were making. Remember, blind them, don't bother hitting them." She made a call on the spot. "If we get separated, we meet at the plaza."

Everyone knew where the plaza was, but not everyone knew where Hazel lived. Di handed her a kitchen knife. They passed shoes around in a disorganized mess.

Without waiting for Morgan's consent, Hazel opened the door.

Barricade

There was a growl at the sight of the girls, and the nearest monster broke into a sprint. Hazel decided to outrun it. She darted down the little stairs and across the dark front lawns to the right. Jen kept pace behind her. Nearby growls told her the two of them had drawn the most attention. She imagined the other girls running in a second wave, going unnoticed behind the zombies. She and Jen would have to run just slow enough that the monsters didn't give up and turn around.

"I'll go on ahead," Kelly said, and Hazel saw that she was moving faster through her new state than by her own feet, almost like she was gliding along a walkway at the airport. In the past, Kelly would have struggled to keep up. "I'll see if there's anything to watch out for."

"Me too," said Breanna, with a determined nod.

Hazel experienced a moment of panic; if Kelly reached the limit of how far she could go from her body, Hazel might never see her again. She hadn't even warned Breanna this could happen. In her selfish desire to keep her sister, Hazel had neglected to do what she did with all ghosts that crossed her path. She hadn't guided them into letting go. How terrible if either Breanna or Kelly found themselves wandering the living world alone. In the seconds it took Hazel to feel guilt and panic, the ghosts were gone.

She couldn't ignore that the shoes she wore were imprinted with someone else's feet. Her heel still felt tender from jumping out of the French room. In running for her life, she realized how many inconveniences and emotions could hinder her. Her pursuers were invincible in comparison. The growling was close behind. She tried to shove it all aside, but was left with the blinding fear of death. She latched onto the open air; she was free of that wretched house and the evil shadow.

Then Kelly was back. "Take a right ahead. Most of them are after you and Jen. You should steer them away from the others so they have a clear path to the plaza."

Hazel reached the corner of the block and made a chopping motion with her hand to indicate the other girls should carry on straight ahead.

Jen followed her. "You're going the wrong way!"

"So are the zombies," she explained with a nod to their followers.

"You can loop around the back of the plaza," Kelly continued, "and hopefully ditch them behind it. Only thing is there's an abandoned barricade of cars and junk, and some of the corrupt are down at the bottom. On our side."

Hazel repeated the plan to Jen in as few words as she could manage.

"How do you know that?"

"Kelly told me!"

"But—"

"What are we going to do about the barricade?" she interrupted, speaking to Kelly.

"The corrupt at the bottom are the bigger problem," Kelly

said. "You can climb the barricade."

"Perfect," Hazel said. "What do you suggest for the zombies?"

She was aware of Jen staring, but ignored her.

She put on an extra burst of speed as a new monster arrived from a side street and lunged at her. It stumbled and fell, almost taking out Jen as it went down. She dodged it, but Hazel could hear her straining to keep up.

"I have an idea," Breanna said, appearing at Hazel's elbow. "It's crude."

"What is it?"

"Get the other girls to smash a window. An alarm should go off."

"But the zombies will go after them!"

"You just need enough time to get up onto the roof and break in. The dollar store had roof access. All the stores are the same. You can climb the barricade to get up there."

"Watch the other girls," Kelly said to Breanna. "Then you can tell us when the timing is right and Hazel can yell for them to smash it."

Breanna steered off in the opposite direction. Hazel shook her head, her stomach turning with nerves.

"One thing at a time," Kelly advised. "Right now you need to stall the corrupt long enough for the others to make it to the store."

"Backup plan?" Hazel asked. "What if we get trapped in the store?"

"Then you'll have to fight them off," Kelly said, looking grim. "You have more than desks this time."

"Hazel?" Jen asked. She sounded like she was wondering who she had hitched herself to.

Hazel repeated the information. "Don't think about it," she panted. "Just concentrate."

Hazel could hear the heavy breathing of the zombies behind them. Without looking she guessed there were at least six to be most concerned about. She saw Jen look back again and fall behind a little more.

"'Don't look down,' Jen!" she called over her shoulder. It must have been a line from a movie, but Hazel had no idea why it would occur to her now.

"Right," Jen panted, her voice a squeak.

Hazel counted the blocks before the left turn to the plaza. They would be running full tilt for a good twenty minutes, and they would feel the pain before the zombies. She started to worry.

"Go right," Kelly said, "circle around the block to get back here."

Hazel obeyed. "Why?"

"Did you see those ones lurking around ahead? This way they'll chase after you and clear the way."

"Hazel," Jen called, "we're going to burn out if we keep doing this."

"If we burn out we die," she replied. "Don't burn out."

"Oh god," Jen wheezed.

Hazel chanced a glance back and saw the new zombies joining the chase. One of them was fast.

"Pick it up!"

Jen groaned, twisted her face in a grimace of effort, and pushed off harder against the ground. Hazel let her draw level. The gardening hoe stabbed at the air with the pumping of Jen's arms. Hazel could see the sweat sparkling on her forehead. By the time they rounded the block, Hazel's breath burned in her throat. She coughed, then choked. Jen had no words left, and exhaustion wore away at her determined look. They raced through the neighbourhood, taking alleys and cutting through parking lots. Finally, they could see the plaza's boring beige paint and heavy back doors ahead. There was one last street to go.

"Almost there," Kelly said. "Time to cue the other girls."

"How?" Hazel asked, still hacking. "Can't—breathe."

Cluing in, Jen shoved two fingers into her mouth and blew a shrill blast that screeched against the walls around them. Hazel cringed.

"Riva! Morgan!" Jen screamed. "Break glass! Make noise! Alexis! Di! Break something NOW!"

She was winded. Hazel grabbed her by the elbow and pulled her along. Kelly ran ahead again. As they came closer and closer to the plaza with no sound of shattering glass, Hazel's terror multiplied. She and Jen might die in a backstreet surrounded by zombies.

"Riva! Break the glass!" she screamed, hoping Riva was on the other side of the building.

At last, an almost musical smash rent the air, followed by screams. Hazel and Jen threw each other looks of horror. There was no alarm. They had forgotten about the power outage.

"You're good!" Kelly shouted, waving them along like a frantic crossing guard. "Come on, come on!"

Ahead was the barrier of cars and discarded furniture. The street was empty except for patches of red that seeped into the cracks of the pavement. Hazel looked up at the apartment building on the right and wondered if anyone was alive in there to help.

Hazel pushed Jen in front of her. "This is it. As hard as you can!"

Jen grunted, but couldn't move faster. Even if she soared up the barricade, Hazel would have to wait for her turn below. She gripped the knife in her hand, feeling sweat slip down the handle. Adrenaline made her eyes dart left and right. There was a growl in her ear.

Jen didn't slow down at the barricade. In one great bound she leapt onto the side mirror of the police car and pushed off it. It snapped. She fell with one knee on the car, the other dangling. The gardening hoe clattered to the ground. Hazel came to an abrupt halt, using the side of the car as a brace. Jen dragged herself up, but her fall shifted the debris. A filing cabinet tipped over the back of the car, crashing to the ground with a sonorous boom. In another moment, Jen disappeared behind a bookshelf.

Hazel spun around and slid her knife across the eyes and nose of the zombie at her tail. Even in the chaos of the moment, she wanted to puke. She ducked and went right so that the now blind monster waved its arms against the car, thinking she was still there. The next one was already upon her. Hazel rolled sideways against the car and lost some time.

"Kelly!" she cried, though her sister could do nothing.

An office chair came flying over the barricade and knocked the advancing zombie down. Hazel backed into the plaza wall, the last zombie-free space, the concrete cold against her bare arms. Debris kept launching at the monsters, but half of it smashed on the ground. Jen couldn't see what she was doing.

"Run!" Kelly screamed.

Natural Life

It was the only option. She turned back the way she had come. She would have to lead the zombies away and try again. She barreled through the oncoming monsters, feeling the fingernails graze her arm. She swung her knife, trying to imitate that first double-eye blinding in one stroke. She could hear screaming, but it seemed to come from everywhere.

Then Riva came charging around the corner, rake straight out in front of her like a zombie-snowplow. Most of the corrupt were pouring from the alley perpendicular to the plaza, so there was only a small group separating Riva and Hazel. Riva shoved and steered the corrupt from behind, taking them by surprise and making a brief path. Hazel jumped over the tangle of legs and clawing arms, dragging Riva back through the path with her. She was too relieved to ask how Riva had found her.

"This way!" Riva said, directing Hazel towards the front of the plaza.

"We'll lead them right to everyone!" Hazel gasped between breaths that felt like rips in her lungs.

Riva didn't have time to answer as zombies emptied out of the surrounding streets, attracted by all the noise.

"Up!" Riva said, pointing to the plaza roof.

Hazel followed her finger and saw a zig-zagging rain pipe.

"Are you kidding me?" she cried.

Riva ran to the wall and started to climb, rake tucked into the crook of her elbow and the prongs hooked over her shoulder. Hazel kept on straight ahead. Running was her strength, not climbing.

"Hazel!" she heard Riva calling, aghast.

Hazel put Riva out of her mind, knowing she would be alright if she climbed fast enough. Most of the zombies were too bloody to climb a pole without slipping. Breanna and Kelly appeared at her sides, both talking at the same time.

"Why didn't you take the drain pipe?" Kelly cried.

"There's too many of them! Go back!" Breanna said.

"Some of them got in the store, it's not safe in there!"

Hazel swore as the gap between the nearest zombie and the corner of the building narrowed. She pulled in her arms and tried to zip between them. The zombie's grabbing hand tore at her shirt just before her shoulder blasted into him and sent him spinning. She made the corner and dodged right, grazing the front of the dollar store. Natural Life was in the middle of the building. There was a sparkle of glass on the sidewalk out front. There was also Jen, swinging a flat-screen TV from the barricade as a shield. Like, Riva, she hadn't been able to leave Hazel alone. She was facing a woman whose back teeth showed between strips of cheek. Three more attackers descended upon her, one coming from inside the store.

"No!" Jen sobbed.

"Jen!"

"Hazel! Help me!"

It was like a nightmare Hazel had once had, where she was running from a clown, but her feet were melting into the sticky cement. Her thighs burned and wouldn't listen to her brain's call of 'faster!' She threw her knife. It whizzed past the head of the old man zombie, distracting him only for a second. The woman pushed against the TV, gnawing at Jen's knuckles as she backed towards both the glass and the zombie from the store.

Jen fell. She shrunk under the TV in a last defence, the TV wobbling over her body like the shell of a turtle. Hazel threw herself at the woman in a football tackle. They knocked down the old man she had almost impaled. Hazel rolled away and scrambled up, stumbling and exhausted, but ready to attack the zombie from the store. He was kneeling down with his hands outstretched for Jen's face, mouth already open. Hazel lunged.

The tackle was pathetic, spent as she was. The zombie grabbed her bare neck as they went down. It was only for a split-second, but Hazel's hands and feet went cold. The woman zombie descended upon her as well. There was a terror so deep she felt a hole in her stomach, where dread gathered and contaminated the rest of her body. She lost track of what she was doing and scraped her arm on the pavement. She saw a flash of herself cornered, but then the zombies released her and the vision faded.

Jen was up. She smashed the TV down over the two zombies' heads as Hazel recoiled. The old man zombie was reaching for Jen from behind. Jen grabbed Hazel's hand and hauled her to her feet. Without letting go, Hazel pulled Jen away and aimed a kick at the oncoming zombie's shin. The timing was perfect and the zombie collapsed like Hazel had kicked out the leg of a table. Both girls danced away from the hands at their ankles.

All around them, zombies were arriving. The girls dove into Natural Life through the broken window. Moonlight stopped short of the tills. There was a growl from the depths of the store. Hazel motioned to Jen to duck behind an aisle.

"I counted three," she whispered.

"The ones outside are coming in too."

They crept past a selection of sparkling rocks and gems to the middle of the store, where there was a break in the aisles. Hazel peered around the corner. One zombie was rattling a door towards the back of the store. Hazel guessed the girls had taken the lavender up to the rooftop. A second zombie was near the till, looking down aisles for where they had gone. The third one Hazel could only hear. It was blundering around behind them in the next aisle.

They had to move fast. The corrupt were pouring in from outside, some running down the middle of the store as if they were going too fast to stop. Hazel grabbed a handful of clear crystal quartz stones. Jen copied. The rocks made a gentle clinking that seemed much louder than it should have been. Hazel drew back her arm and stood up, Jen mimicking her. They aimed at the far corner of the store, at the front, and released.

The quartz clattered and banged like gunfire against the metaphysical paraphernalia. The zombies turned as one and rushed the spot. Jen and Hazel pressed against the shelves to hide as the zombie from the next aisle ran past. Hazel had the sudden urge to pee, like when she played hide-and-seek as a kid. She fought the sensation down. When the way was clear, they scurried in a crouch across the gap to the back aisles. Hazel cast a furtive glance at the zombies and saw a fight break out over the non-existent bodies.

Just around a corner, in a narrow hallway, was the door to the roof.

Jen moved to pass Hazel, saying, "I'll check it."

"Wait," Hazel whispered back, stopping her with a hand on the shoulder. "Are we sure they got the lavender?"

Breanna made Hazel flinch, arriving in the walkway without bothering to hide. "They got that stuff."

She pointed to the shelves behind them, where there was a selection of incense and bundles of dried plants for various ailments.

"Which one did they take?" Hazel asked, but she already knew something was wrong.

"Alexis and Di just grabbed handfuls of stuff. They were all being chased."

"What is it?" Jen asked, checking on the zombies again.

"The lavender braids are a few aisles over," Hazel said. "Closer to the zombies. It's more popular than this stuff so they put it in a better spot."

"So?"

Hazel had lost track of what Jen could hear. "The girls grabbed stuff from here instead."

"We can't risk it," Jen said, shaking her head. "Let's get out of here."

"We didn't do this for nothing," Hazel argued.

"We did it to get away from that thing in the house. We're away." Jen moved to leave.

Hazel grabbed her arm. "It can come after us. It came after my Gran. I saw it in the hospital." Before Jen could argue, Hazel said, "I'll go get it, I know where it is. You get us through that door as fast as you can."

Jen gave the locked door a worried look.

Breanna opened her mouth to speak, but Hazel interrupted. "Wait, where's Kelly?"

Breanna bit her lip. "I don't know."

"Kelly? Your sister was here?" Jen asked.

They heard footsteps and turned to see a corrupt man sprinting towards them, drooling blood. They scattered. Jen ducked into the hallway with the door, and Hazel bolted to the lavender aisle, whipped into it, and actually held her breath.

With her back against the metal shelves, Hazel resisted checking if the corrupt man was coming. She spotted the braids a little ways in, and slid sideways towards them. She grabbed the biggest bundle she could find of the brittle, purple and green plant. It was wrapped with a string from stems to leaves. It was as long as her forearm. Hazel usually only used a small braid for her whole house, but there was no telling how much she would need to get rid of the shadow. She grabbed another two bundles and shoved them under her arms, while her eyes flitted to both ends of the aisle.

The drooling man appeared at the same time as several more corrupt at the opposite end of the aisle. They had lost interest in the quartz. She was cornered. Before Hazel could do more than process the trouble she was in, both parties were racing to get to her first. In desperation, Hazel ran at the lone zombie. Head down, she let out a nervous scream as she hammered into his legs, raising him up and flipping him over her back. She was shocked when he tumbled onto his head behind her. Not for the first time, Hazel was grateful for her body.

She turned on her heel and ran to join Jen at the door to the rooftop. Her borrowed shoes squealed to a halt in the hallway. Jen was gone.

Rooftop

The corrupt were at her back.

"Jen?" Hazel cried, giving up on sneaking altogether.

"The door!" Breanna said.

Hazel yanked at the door handle. It didn't open. She turned to run left into the back of the store where there might be a bathroom to hide in, but just then the door opened without her help. Someone grabbed the back of her shirt. Hazel choked as she was yanked onto a set of stairs. She snapped some of the lavender under her elbow as she crashed to the steps, crushing someone's leg under her as she went. The door slammed shut.

"Lock it! Lock it!" someone cried.

Hazel was blind in the darkness. She pushed herself back up, and felt the leg withdraw. There was the click of a bolt.

"Who's there?" Hazel asked.

"Morgan and Jen," Morgan replied.

"Thank god you're okay," came Kelly's whimper.

Hazel went weak with relief at the sound of her sister's voice. "Where have you been?"

"You're welcome," Morgan scoffed. "We found a door to the roof and were trying to watch out for you."

"I didn't mean it like that," Hazel corrected. "I was worried about you."

Morgan didn't answer, but Hazel sensed she was mollified.

"Jen? You okay?"

"I'm good," Jen replied. "Was that the lavender?"

"Yeah, but it should be fine."

"Well grab it, we need to move fast," Morgan said.

Hazel felt around on the dark steps and scooped up two bundles while Jen retrieved the third. The zombies pounded on the door. Morgan led the way up the stairs, her shoes making grinding sounds as if bits of glass were stuck to the soles. Hazel's thighs burned as she climbed, and she fell behind. Then they opened an outer door, ascended a few more steps, and emerged onto the roof.

"Hazel!" Riva cried from where she was staring over the edge of the plaza. She rushed Hazel and buried her in hug. "I'm so glad you're okay."

Hazel shook as she squeezed her back. They exchanged teary nods when they pulled away. Alexis and Di, who had also been looking over the edge, joined them. Both girls looked too sick with fright and relief to speak. It was Jen who surprised Hazel with the next embrace. Jen had never hugged her like this before. Hazel's heart, already overworked, stopped for a moment.

"I thought you were dead when I broke the car mirror."

"Oh." Hazel's brain seemed to have skipped a pulse too.

"We have to go," Morgan said from way down at the end of the building. "The drain pipe is dry enough."

Jen and Hazel gave the others questioning looks.

"The corrupt got it all bloody chasing Riva, so they couldn't get a grip. But they got onto the house; they can get up here too."

"We can't get down through the barricade either," Alexis

said. "There're more trying to climb it. They know we're up here."

"We have to get back to the house," Morgan said, as if continuing an argument. "It's already barricaded. We can't start over."

"We were almost out of food," Riva said.

"Then we should break into the dollar store and get some. And then we can sneak out the front. The corrupt in the weirdo store and on the drain pipe won't even notice."

"It's a good place to start," Di said to Riva.

"We have to go home," Alexis chipped in. "I sent out our address. That's where rescue will go if it's coming."

Riva sighed and they took that as assent. Alexis led the way to the dollar store and down the stairwell to the locked door.

"How did you break through the last door?" Hazel asked.

"It was unlocked," Riva answered. "Someone else escaped this way."

"Morgan?" Di interrupted.

Morgan had gone to check on the corrupt's progress up the drain pipe. Now she was swinging her legs over, clinging to the wall for balance. She made a kicking motion. There was a roar followed by a thud.

"We have a bit more time," she called back.

Hazel assessed the tools available to them: lavender, a knife, a rake, and the cultivator.

"Try the rake," Kelly said.

Hazel passed the suggestion on to Di, who grabbed the rake and wedged the prongs into the crack just under the door handle. She gave it a solid kick to make sure it was all the way in place.

"There isn't enough room to push on it," Di said, but she squeezed between the rake's handle and the door anyway.

She turned sideways so that her hip pushed out the handle. Alexis grabbed the rake from the other side and pulled. There was a small cracking sound.

"Did we even make a gap?" Di asked. There was pain in her voice as the rake dug into her hipbone. "Can we fit anything into it? The handle's going to snap."

Alexis retrieved the cultivator and imitated Di by wedging it above the door handle and kicking it in place. Di ducked out from behind the rake, which hovered in the air like a flag. There was another roar and thud in the distance.

"I keep knocking 'em back," Morgan sang. She might have been playing a video game and winning.

"Pull the rake this time," Alexis said, "and I'll push the other thing."

With her back to the wall, Alexis used the end of the rake as a prop for her foot and shimmied up the wall until she could get her shoe behind the little cultivator. Di heaved at the rake. Alexis bounced a few times against the gardening tool, straining. This time there was a loud, splintering crack, and the tools clattered to the ground. Alexis fell in a heap to the floor, scraping her face on the way down.

"Are you okay?" Di gasped, rushing to help her up.

Alexis touched her scratched cheek, but said, "I'm fine." She inspected the frame. "The wood in the frame is starting to break, but the deadbolt's still in there."

She set up the tools again and climbed back up with Di steadying the now loose rake.

"I need the rake!" Morgan called. "They're grabbing at my feet!"

Riva called back, "Just a little longer!"

Hazel peeked around the stairs to check on Morgan. Her

movements were different. She was aiming with caution and pulling her leg back fast between kicks. Hazel hurried over to see if she could help. When she looked over the edge, she gasped. Four of the corrupt were on the pipe, two of them vying for Morgan's foot at the top. One managed to grab her shoe. Morgan kicked straight up to get free, and almost toppled over backwards onto the roof. Hazel steadied her.

"Hurry!" Morgan yelled over her shoulder.

She did a double take, and Hazel followed her gaze. A zombie was pulling itself onto the roof from the barricade. There was a crunch and scrape from the stairwell, followed by cries of pain. Hazel and Morgan abandoned the wall and raced to join the girls. Di had caught Alexis this time, and both girls were lying on the ground groaning. The door opened onto darkness. There was a moment of silence as all the girls paused to listen, but if there were zombies in there, they didn't come running.

Alexis reached out to pick up the cultivator. "Not such a useless tool now, is it?"

Morgan flapped her hands in a gesture for quiet. "They're coming!"

Jen snatched up the rest of the scattered tools from the steps. There was pushing and stumbling as all the girls scrambled down the stairs. Morgan slammed the door shut.

"We broke the locks, what can we use?"

Everyone looked at the collection of objects in Jen's arms.

"We need those for the door at the bottom of the stairs," Breanna said, and Hazel repeated.

"Then go!" Morgan yelled. She clung to the handle with both hands and stuck a foot on each side of the door frame.

"Here," Riva said, leaving a knife on the landing.

Di thudded into the door at the bottom and shook the handle.

She groaned. "It opens out!"

"Maybe we can kick it down," Jen said, dumping the tools and lavender into Riva's arms. "Look out."

Jen aimed a kick next to the handle. The boom was echoed upstairs by the corrupt crashing into the door.

"Again!" Di said.

Jen kicked a few more times, her face screwed up with effort. The door rattled, but nothing more. At last, panting, she motioned for someone else to try. Hazel took her spot on the first step. She slammed her foot against the wood, leaning all her weight into it. It vibrated so hard there was a twanging sound.

"Hurry up!" Morgan cried, sounding desperate.

"We're trying!"

"Come on, Hazel," Breanna said. "You can do it."

She tried again. The door inched forward.

"Come on," Alexis begged, her words muffled by the fingernails in her mouth.

Hazel struck again. BOOM. The door shifted again. BOOM. It wedged in place and wouldn't move further.

"Morgan's losing it," Kelly called. "They're getting their hands in the crack."

They heard Morgan swear from the darkness of the landing.

"Someone try it with me," Hazel panted, gripping the railing for support.

Jen was back, in line with Hazel on the first step.

"One, two, three," they rattled off.

The door finally flew open, wooden shrapnel flying from the frame into the store.

"Now, Morgan!" Riva said, as the girls flew inside, one after the other.

There was a gasp upstairs and the sound of the knife clacking down the steps. Alexis let out a yelp as the growling-dog sound filled the stairwell. Morgan leapt down six steps as Alexis prepared to slam the door, but in the dark she landed on the knife. She went head first down the last stairs, rolling and banging until she was through the frame. Di and Hazel grabbed her arms and dragged her in. Alexis flung the door shut in the first zombie's face.

"Here," Riva cried, wheeling over a stock trolley laden with heavy boxes.

Alexis slipped out of the way so Riva and Jen could line it up and engage the brakes. The corrupt pounded against the other side of door, unable to make it budge.

Plans

"**M**organ, are you alright?" Hazel asked as Morgan curled up, holding her arm.

She nodded, but her face paled as she clenched her eyes shut. Riva took up the rake and prowled the store in search of hidden attackers. Jen headed for the front window to spy on the zombies still out there.

"We're clear," Riva called after a minute.

Di and Alexis were already rummaging around the store to find the food they needed.

Alexis' voice carried over from a few aisles to the right. "Oh thank god, toilet paper."

Morgan winced as she sat up. "That's going to leave a huge bruise," she muttered, touching her good hand to her hip.

"Can she move her fingers?" Kelly asked.

Hazel played nurse again. She had Morgan wiggle her fingers, but Morgan gave a sharp intake of breath.

"I'm thinking something's broken," Kelly confirmed. "Although it could be sprained. It's hard to tell. That's what x-rays are for."

"Okay, try not to move it much," Hazel said. "We'll see if we can find a medical kit or something that might help."

"Pain killers," Morgan replied.

"I'll get it," Jen offered, returning from the front window.

"Morgan, will you be okay while I go see if we can get organized?" Hazel asked.

Morgan nodded, her eyes on the still rattling door. Hazel left and found Alexis and Riva arguing about how to carry everything they wanted.

"A shopping cart would be too loud, we need backpacks," Riva said.

"Backpacks are too heavy," Alexis returned. "We need to be able to run."

"And who's going to be the sacrifice who has to push a cart that weighs more than them?"

"It's got wheels! We managed when we had to wheel Hazel—"

"Hazel," Riva interrupted, spotting her coming down the school supplies aisle, "what do you think? Shopping carts or backpacks?"

Hazel frowned. "Backpacks."

"Why?" Alexis argued. "A zombie could grab your backpack and you'd be screwed. But you can abandon a shopping cart if you have to. And we're going to be chased anyway, what does it matter if it's two or ten chasing us?"

"We could get so much further if we can sneak—"

"That's not guaranteed," Alexis said.

"If we all take backpacks at least some supplies will make it back," Hazel pointed out, "even if we have to ditch a few bags."

Alexis sighed and gave in. They set off shopping, getting creative at the same time as thinking practically about their needs. They stuffed a cart full of non-perishable foods, lighters, candles, flashlights, medical supplies, rope, toiletries, and hygiene products. They also armed themselves with kitchen knives that came with different coloured plastic sheaths. Riva found some small backpacks and loaded them with a bit of each item. When they were done, they gathered at the back of the store.

"What's the plan?" Jen asked.

Alexis rattled off the ideas they had, but Hazel glanced at Morgan. She had her head against the wall, was still pale, and looked like she might fall asleep any minute.

"Is now the best time to go?" Hazel asked. "We already ran really far today, and now Morgan's injured..."

What she didn't voice was her dread of returning to the shadow. By the way the others avoided the subject, Hazel knew they were all thinking about it too.

"I'm not dead," Morgan said, but her lack of eye contact suggested she would be relieved if they didn't go tonight.

Di massaged her thighs and argued in favour of leaving right away. "We're going to be sore tomorrow. Or at least, I know I am."

"What about my text?" Alexis said. "I sent out our address. For all we know, rescue could be there right now."

There was an uncomfortable silence at that.

"I think we're going to have to risk missing them," Hazel said. "Realistically, if we go out tonight, some of us are going to die."

Alexis chewed her nails. Jen shifted from foot to foot.

"We can go when it's still dark," Riva suggested. "Really early in the morning. That way we get some rest, but we'll still have the advantage, and we won't be away from home for that long."

"You can always try to send another message," Di said to Alexis. "Right?"

Alexis grimaced and gave a non-comital shrug.

"And what about the...you know..." Riva said, eyeing the finger-shaped welts on her arm.

"We're going to take care of that," Hazel said, inserting a confidence she didn't feel into her voice. "We'll get rid of the hooks. We've got the lavender."

"The hooks? What hooks?"

Hazel had forgotten she hadn't shared that part with everyone. She hesitated.

"What do you know?" Riva asked, giving Hazel an intense stare.

"Well..." Hazel took a deep breath to slow her heart. It was still scary to talk about ghosts out loud. She had been avoiding it her whole life. "Breanna and Kelly talked to a dead man outside Jen's... That's why I messed up on how many corrupt were outside the house," she explained, trying to give them some proof. "I forgot I was seeing ghosts as well. But they wouldn't come inside. The man said they're afraid of the shadow. It has hooks in everyone."

"What does that mean?" Riva frowned.

Hazel swallowed. Her best friend was looking at her with mingled worry, disbelief, and calculation. She was struggling to believe her.

A little panicked, Hazel continued, "I don't know, exactly. It seems like the shadow is sort of...thriving on all the death around here. Like...eating it up, in a way. We're like fish it's caught. We're on its hooks."

"No matter where we are?" Alexis said into the quiet that followed.

"I know you don't want to believe it, it's so awful," Hazel said, wringing her hands, "but just because it's awful doesn't mean it's not true. We have to get rid of the shadow, for everyone. Alive, and dead."

"We know ghosts are real," Riva said to the others at last. She swallowed. "And when the thing grabbed my arm I-I saw things. Visions." She nodded to Alexis. "Like you did when the zombie touched you. I-I think they are connected."

"You should have seen us running from the corrupt," Jen added. "Hazel knew stuff she couldn't have known."

After another pause, Alexis turned to Hazel and said, "I have so many questions for you."

Hazel gave her a blank stare. There was fear, but also curiosity in Alexis' eyes. Hazel remembered the night her own mother said ghosts didn't exist. She felt an unexpected rush of affection for the girl in black sneakers and a skirt. Tears prickled her eyes, and she smiled at her feet.

Medium

They settled in for the night. Di gathered soft items like tiny throws and dog beds to sleep on. Riva broke into tills and the office, searching for spare keys to unlock the bars over the front door in the morning. Meanwhile, Hazel found a tiny alarm clock which she stuffed batteries into and set for 4:00am. Morgan popped painkillers from the staff room and pounded back water after water.

They decided the office was the safest place for them to spend the night. It had a derelict staff washroom next door and a tiny barred window high on the wall which looked out into the alley. Jen moved the heavy desk up against the trolley in the hall for added protection. Alexis even found apples in the staff room, which she collected and shared out. She also found ramen noodles which they crunched on as a dry second dinner.

"When this is over we're going to owe this dollar store a lot of money," said Jen, who was opening a can of peaches with a brand new can opener.

Hazel was using duct tape to strap knives to broom handles. She wanted distance from the visions next time she had to take out a zombie's eyes. She waited until the screeching zip of unraveling tape ended before she asked, "When do you think it'll be over?"

"I guess it depends on why it happened," Jen answered through a mouthful, "and how far it got. Like, if it's bacteria in the water or in the food... That would be bad. But if it's something easier to contain then they should be rescuing people now. Right?"

Hazel shrugged and smoothed a stray bit of duct tape over the broom handle. "Unless they think we're all contaminated too. Then they might leave us 'til they know."

Jen finished a few more bites before she said, "Anyway. I'd like to know how things went for 'B' team."

"'B' team?" Riva scoffed from her perch at the window. "You mean the people who saved you at least twice?"

Jen grinned. "So what happened?"

The girls shared their experience of racing to the plaza. It turned out Morgan managed to stay so calm that she saved both Di and Riva in separate attacks. Alexis was the one who heard Jen and Hazel screaming to break the window, which she did with a metal garbage can. Then they escaped to the roof and Riva saw Hazel in trouble at the barricade, so she climbed down to the rescue. Everyone had escaped with a few bites and scratches, but nothing fatal.

When the girls had finished their food and settled on their dog beds and under throws, Alexis spoke again.

"Can you see ghosts right now, Hazel?"

"Yes. Just two."

"Breanna and Kelly?"

"Mhm."

"A-are they okay?"

Hazel looked to the ghosts. Kelly was sitting on the desk with her feet dangling, and Breanna was laying down with her head propped on her hand behind Morgan. They exchanged a look.

"We're as okay as we can be, considering we're dead," Kelly said, but her tone was gentle.

Breanna piped up, "Tell them we're so glad they're okay, and we miss talking to them."

Hazel repeated both.

Tears blossomed in Alexis' eyes. She hesitated, then asked, "Does...Breanna...blame us?"

"Of course not," Breanna said, shaking her head. "I wish things went differently... But I-I'm the one who wasn't fast enough."

"No one was prepared for this," Hazel told her. "It's not your fault. It could have been any one of us. It's just how it...played out." To the other girls she said, "She blames herself, not us."

The girls raised objections all at the same time, talking over each other, whether they believed Hazel or not. Tears spilled down Breanna's cheeks and disappeared before they hit Morgan's blanket.

"This is so wonderful," she said, wiping at her eyes.

"And Kelly," Di said, "tell Kelly we miss her too."

She was so eager that Hazel's heart ached for her. "You just told her."

"She can hear me?"

Hazel nodded.

Di sobbed and said, "I love you, Kelly."

Kelly chewed her lips and tried not to cry.

"She was there that night," Hazel said, "after she died, and you were crying. She wanted so bad to talk to you. But I knew you wouldn't believe me."

"I believe you now," Di said, her chin quivering.

"Can you talk to anyone?" Riva asked.

"Anyone who comes to me," Hazel said.

"My grandmother...?"

Hazel gave a sympathetic shake of the head. "I hoped she would, but she never did. She was ready to go, and she knew what to do. Usually when they find me they're still in shock, or they need help."

"Kelly and Breanna?" asked Di.

Both ghosts avoided Hazel's eye.

"That's a tough question," Hazel said, choosing not to force an answer out of them.

"Could they find my grandmother?" Riva persisted.

Hazel turned to the girls again. She didn't know the answer.

Kelly shook her head. "I wouldn't know where to start. We don't leave traces."

"I don't think she stuck around anyways," Hazel agreed. "She probably went on to heaven, or whatever." To Riva she said, "Ghosts can travel our world as long as they stay near their bodies. So if your grandmother stayed around, Kelly and Breanna could run into her. But she was ready to go. You know that...right?"

Riva nodded, but Hazel could feel her disappointment stinging as if chopped onions were in the air. Gran had never visited either.

"So since Breanna and Kelly found you, will they stay with you forever?" Di asked.

Hazel opened her mouth and closed it again. Her pause stretched on for too long. Kelly sat up straighter.

"I wish they could," Hazel mumbled.

"What do you mean by that?" Kelly asked.

"Why can't they?" Di asked at the same time.

Hazel sighed and struggled to find the right words. "It's not right."

Everyone else frowned.

"Ghosts who stick around get frustrated. They can't talk to anyone. Mediums, like me, end up in charge of passing on what they say, or not, so they have no control. And then I would feel guilty for trying to live my life; I can't run around passing out messages from the-the beyond or whatever. I'm not just a telephone, I'm a person, it's...it's hard for everyone."

Di looked in Kelly's direction. After a moment, she said, "Sounds like it would be worth it though."

"Yeah," Kelly agreed, and there was a hint of defiance in her voice.

"You can't live through someone else," Hazel said to her, pleading with her eyes. "Think about how lonely that would be."

Kelly got up and walked out through the wall into the alley.

Encircled

T he alarm blared, shocking the entire group from sleep to sitting up. Riva fumbled with the plastic clock, sending it flying into Alexis' lap, who panicked and pulled the batteries out. There were stars outside the barred window, and not even weak morning light. Breanna flew to the bars to check if they had been exposed.

"We're okay," she said after a pause.

Hazel repeated the message and everyone unfroze. Morgan was clutching her arm, which she had used to sit up.

"Gaaaawd," Alexis groaned, thumping back onto her cushion. "It's so early…"

"Don't make me do this again," Morgan said, and there was a break in her voice. "I'm so tired."

Worried, Hazel studied Morgan's pallor. Almost nothing had ruffled Morgan since the initial attack at school. She looked around for Kelly, but her sister had still not returned.

"We have to," Hazel said, climbing across the make-shift beds to get to Morgan's side. "Here," she handed her the bottle of pills and water bottle that rested next to her. "Did you get much sleep?"

"It doesn't feel like it," Morgan said, and she buried her face in her knees.

Hazel didn't know what to say. "Can I get you anything?"

Morgan shook her head, but didn't look up. Hazel grimaced at Riva, across the room.

"Let's get ready," Riva said.

They left the room together, peeking out in the hallway where the air was chilly to see if the coast was clear.

"She's probably just exhausted," Riva whispered when they were in the staff room. "She'll feel better when she wakes up."

"I hope so. We need everyone alert."

Breanna had followed them in.

"Where's Kelly?" Hazel asked.

"I don't know. She hasn't come back."

Hazel felt a stab of fear.

"What's the matter?" asked Riva.

"It's probably nothing," Hazel said.

But she wasn't sure. Hazel went to the sink and splashed water on her face, more terrified that she had chased her sister away forever than she was to face the corrupt again.

With backpacks on and broom-handle spears at the ready, they gathered in the office among the debris of sleeping gear.

"Ready?" Riva asked, and Hazel saw her hand shake as she reached for the door handle.

They crept through the darkened aisles. There was a light rustle of plastic wrapping that lifted from where it hung on shelves as they passed. Riva and Hazel approached the front door at a crouch. Together, they looked out at the empty street.

"Why's it so quiet?" Riva asked.

"I don't even see ghosts," Hazel said, unnerved.

"What does that mean?"

"I don't know. I've seen them every day since this thing started."

"Should we just...go?"

Hazel thought for a moment. "It feels like a trap. But that can't be right."

"I think we should go." Riva turned back to the others. "Do you think we should go?"

"Might as well take advantage," said Morgan, who was indeed looking rosier now that she was awake. She had a sling around her neck, but her arm was free of it in case of desperate circumstances.

Riva nodded and used the key she had found to unlock the bars over the door. She slid them to the sides and unlocked the door too. She pushed it open as if she didn't want to stir the air outside. There was a tinkling sound from above and everyone gasped. A little bell hung swaying from the door-frame. Riva stood frozen in the doorway, staring out at the street for signs of movement.

After a while she said, "Still nothing."

She held the door for the others, her make-shift spear clutched in her hand. When everyone was out, they dallied on the sidewalk, thrown off by the complete lack of reception.

"Let's go, I guess," Hazel whispered.

They tiptoed along, eyes darting to the cracks between buildings and even to the roofs. Breanna was off scouting for them, and Hazel felt exposed without a ghost at her side. They kept to the left side of the road so that they could hide against stores, houses, or in bushes if need be. The farther they walked, the less necessary their caution seemed.

"I don't like this," Jen hissed. "They're never this quiet."

"I feel like they're going to jump out at us," Di agreed, checking over her shoulder. "Let's go back."

She stopped in the middle of a sidewalk, and the group

faltered.

"Everyone seemed to agree, so I went along with it," Di whispered quickly, sinking into the shadow of a brick building, "but I have to say something now. Something feels wrong. We should go back, we have enough supplies in the store. When rescue comes we can tell them about the shadow and they can take care of it. I'm sure there's someone better prepared for this than us. Don't you think?"

Hazel wanted to believe it. It would be such a relief to hand over the responsibility. "Who knows the shadow better than me?"

"We don't have time for this," Jen said, her eyes darting around.

"I have to do it myself," Hazel told Di. "I won't be able to relax until I know it can't get us."

"I-I can barely get behind this ghost stuff," Morgan said. Hazel's heart sank. Then Morgan continued, "But we have to look out for each other. Most of the group wants to go, so we all go. Come on, Di, it's too late for this."

She broke into a light jog, and the others followed as if compelled by some migratory instinct. Their backpacks shuffled with each step. They were halfway home when Hazel froze, horrified. Alexis almost walked into her. When she didn't back off, Hazel knew Alexis was just as petrified.

"What is it?" Riva asked, staring down the alley too.

She gasped. A line of zombies faced them, blocking the entire street to the left. Though the sky was only just lightening over the mountain, Hazel could see the dark stains on their clothes, mouths, and hands. Like the zombies, Hazel's whole party froze.

"Do they see us?" Morgan asked through her teeth, doing

her best not to move her lips.

"They're looking right at us," Hazel answered, her voice shaking.

"Why don't they attack?" Alexis said, holding onto Hazel's backpack for support.

"Should we run?" Riva asked as the standoff went on.

"I think so," Di chipped in.

"On three," Jen said. "One...two...three..."

They broke into a sprint as one, backpacks now jumping on their backs, the contents clinking. They made it to the next road, where the line of corrupt continued, and still not one of them moved.

"What the hell?" Morgan said to no one in particular.

She slowed back down to a walk.

"Morgan," Riva said, "come on, let's just get out of here. Free pass, come on."

Morgan waved her down, nearing the corner and the zombies.

"Morgan, please!" Di said. "Don't tempt them."

"Their faces are all...glazed."

She took a flashlight from her pocket with her good hand and clicked it on. She shone it down the road until it reached a zombie's feet. Di tugged at her arm, begging her to stop. She raised the light a little further.

The corrupt woman went from glazed to alert, eyes landing on the party. Hazel stopped breathing. The woman still didn't move.

"Let's go," Riva took Morgan by the elbow and pulled her way.

They continued at a jog. Hazel was torn between reaching safety and being back in the house with the shadow that much faster. As taut as her nerves were with this eerie quiet, she preferred it to the life or death sprint of yesterday.

"Do you hear that?" Di asked.

Hazel wasn't paying attention. The ghosts were back. She could see a young woman moving along behind the corrupt, inspecting the row. She yelped when Breanna appeared at her side.

"What?" the entire group asked, spears at the ready.

"It's just Breanna," Hazel said, clutching her heart. "Sorry. She scared the crap out of me."

Morgan muttered something sarcastic about needing fresh dollar store underwear as Breanna shared her news.

"The line goes on for ages, there are so many dead people," she said, and Hazel could see she was upset. "It's a circle."

"A circle around what?"

Breanna winced. "You're in it. The house is in it. And the corrupt behind you are following whenever you move."

Hazel whirled around, but she couldn't see anyone in the distance. "But the shadow chased us out of the house. Why would it want us back?"

Breanna shook her head to say she didn't know. "I'm sorry I took so long to get back to you I–I had to check..."

"Check what?"

Her eyes filled with tears. "Who was dead."

Hazel's face fell. "Oh, Breanna...who?"

Faces and names flashed through Hazel's head: Riva's little brother and sister, Jen's parents, Hazel's wrestling couch, and the worst possibility of all, her mom. Hazel hadn't realized until now that she was still holding onto the possibility.

Breanna shook her head, tears flying off her cheeks. She gulped some air and went on. "Later. I saw living people."

"Where?"

"Behind the circle. They were leaving their houses, sneaking away from the corrupt."

"But we're trapped..." Hazel said, staring at the line of corrupt that separated her from other survivors.

Then she spotted Di running to a house on the right side of the road. Riva called her back in a hiss, but Di ignored her and flew up the front steps. Alexis, Hazel, Jen, Riva, and Breanna all chased after her.

"What are you doing?" Morgan demanded from the road as Di tried the door.

"Can't you hear it?"

"Hear what?"

There was a whimper and scraping from inside. Tears jumped to Di's eyes.

"There's a dog in there! It's probably starving!"

Riva looked like she wanted to rush them on, but didn't have the heart to leave the poor dog.

Alexis threw a glance back at the corrupt. "We'll make a lot of noise if we break in."

Hazel touched the collar still on her wrist and remembered nuzzling Salt's face as a child.

"We can try the back door and the windows first," Di said, and she set to work without wasting another second.

Alexis shrugged at the others and went to help. Hazel went around the back, knowing it would be faster to work together. She was jumpy, checking the shadows at the edges of the yard and imagining monsters there. She found a rock in the flowerbed by the back door that didn't look like it belonged. She picked it up on the off chance there was key underneath, but there wasn't. Disappointed, she went to set it down, but Jen stopped her.

"Open it," she said.

"What?"

"Here," Jen took the rock, lined up her fingernails around the middle, and pulled it open. "We had one of these at my old house."

In a little groove inside the rock was a spare key. Hazel unlocked the door with a grating click. She could hear scampering inside as the dog ran from the front of the house to the back.

"Here!" Jen called to the other girls. "We're in!"

Hazel opened the door and a little copper cocker spaniel dashed out with its tail between its legs. It circled Hazel and Jen, the tucked tail whipping back and forth. It made so much noise it sounded like it was crying.

"You poor thing," Di cried, as she came around the house.

She fell to her knees to hug the dog. It licked her face and crawled onto her lap, knocking her down onto the grass. Di laughed. Something brushed against Hazel's legs. For the second time that night, she yelped.

"Oh," she said, as a brown and black tail wound around her ankles. "It's a cat."

The shaggy cat was staring up at her with wide, glowing eyes. She reached down a hand to stroke its head, but it ducked. Hazel offered it her hand to smell instead.

"Any more of you in there?" she asked.

"Leave the door open," Jen said. "They'll get out and feed themselves if they have to."

The cat warmed up to Hazel and allowed her to pet it. Jen peered into the house.

"They have food dishes, but looks like nothing's left."

"Let's see if there's a bag somewhere," Di said.

"Hurry up," Riva squirmed, but she didn't stop them.

The dog and cat followed Di back inside. She came out a moment later with a leash and a bag of dry dog and cat food under each arm.

"You can't be serious, Di," Morgan said, coming around the side of the house at last. "How are we supposed to look after them?"

"How can we not?" she retorted, pouring out some food for the animals, who gobbled it up. She hooked the leash to the dog's collar. "How should we carry the cat?"

The cat turned out not to be a problem. It followed at their heels in a loping run, never falling too far behind. When they finally reached Jen's house, however, both the cat and dog looked wary. The girls weren't too keen on the house either. They stood at the edge of the lawn, eyeing up the boarded windows, looking for the shadow's eyes in the cracks.

Goodbye

azel's eyes kept getting drawn back to the body on the front lawn. She had forgotten about him when they escaped the house. He wasn't a man after all, but a teenage boy. His posture suggested he had fainted. Brown hair tumbled forward so that she couldn't see his face. Hazel's heart went out to him.

"Are we sure he's dead?" Riva asked, seeing where Hazel was looking.

With an anxious glance back at the house, Hazel bent over the boy and touched his shoulder. He didn't move. She took his arm and rolled him back. His entire face was smeared with blood, and his guts spilled out onto the lawn. Hazel jumped back to avoid wetting her feet, and gagged. He fell onto his face again with an unsympathetic thud.

"He has blood all over his mouth," Hazel choked out. "He was corrupt."

"But he's dead," Alexis repeated.

Hazel backed away from the boy.

"How can he be dead if he was corrupt? Does this mean there's a way to kill them?"

Hazel shook her head, troubled.

"We've got the lavender," she reminded them. "Maybe we

should light it now and take it in with us. Just to be safe."

"Yeah," Di said, who was much more vocal with a dog at her side. "Let's do that. Should we all have some, or...?"

"I'll teach you what I do," Hazel said.

Breanna was watching with an eager expression that made Hazel falter. She had forgotten to point out that the lavender would keep ghosts away. Then anxiety squeezed her chest, like her ribs were a vice clamping down on her lungs. It would keep Kelly away too.

She turned to Breanna, trying with her tone to let her down easy. "This will keep all ghosts away."

She watched Breanna's face go from interested to crestfallen.

"I'm so sorry," she said. "In my experience it lasts for a month, but I've never used this much. I think you could stay outside, but...I don't know. It might be best if..."

"If what?"

"If you move on now."

Breanna squeezed her lips together and stared at the ground. The other girls were motionless, listening to the one sided conversation and the silences in between.

"I'm sorry," Hazel said again. "I wish you could stay with us, but—"

"Wait," Breanna said, her head snapping back up, "I have to tell you something."

Hazel's eyebrows rose in surprise.

"I was going to tell you before. The corrupt... The people I saw who were dead..."

Hazel's heart hammered in a deeper base, a dread sound. The names ran through her head again. "Who?"

"My parents—," Breanna choked, and before she could go on, she broke down.

Hazel pressed her palms to her eyes, then ran them through her hair. This was Breanna's time to break down, not hers. She wanted to hug her, to comfort her, and it was torture to be separated by death, but not by sight or voice.

"It's time to go," she said, and it was a struggle to keep her voice steady. "Can you see that? You need to be with them. You can't be alone like this."

Riva said, "Hazel...," but Di shushed her with a hand on her arm.

"Oh god," Breanna sobbed, clutching her chest, and sinking to her knees at the curb, "it hurts."

"I know." Hazel nodded, and the movement caused the tears she was holding back to slip from her eyes.

She knelt beside the inconsolable ghost, and cried with her; it was the closest she could come to comforting her. Breanna's sobs grew louder and more heart-wrenching before they slowed. Hazel glanced up at the other girls with tears plastered all over her face. Jen and Riva were watching from a one-armed hug. Di was hiding her tears as she stroked the cat. Hazel could make out a glitter of tears in Alexis' eyes as she and Morgan watched the encircling corrupt.

"Picture your mom and dad," Hazel said to Breanna at last, shifting on the rough pavement. "How it would feel to see them again. They're not here anymore, but you don't have to be either. You can go. If it's possible to feel their love again, it's worth it. It's worth the risk."

"What if they're not there? What if I just stop existing?"

"If they're there, you get to be with them. If you stop existing, you don't have to feel this pain anymore. I think that's why it's so hard to lose someone. Because it has to be a relief to let go when it's our turn. It has to be worth the risk, or we'd never go.

So it hurts for a reason."

"What about you? What if I can still help?" Breanna asked, her lips trembling.

Hazel smiled. "We can take care of ourselves now. You've already helped us so much. Go. It's okay."

"But...I don't know how."

"That's the easy part. To go, all you have to do is relax. Like when you're meditating. Let everything else go, and that's what lets you go. It doesn't hurt."

Breanna nodded. More tears ran down her cheeks as she said, "Say goodbye to Kelly for me. To everyone—"

"I will. We owe you."

Breanna shook her head and giggled. "Don't be stupid."

They smiled grateful, watery smiles at each other a moment longer.

"One more thing," Breanna said, and she looked pained to say it. "I saw Alexis' aunt."

Hazel sighed and plucked a strand of grass from the lawn. Alexis and her brother lived with their aunt. They were estranged from their father, and their mother had died when they were young. Her aunt was their only family left.

"Thank you for telling me."

"Are you going to tell her?"

Hazel thought for a moment, then tossed the grass back down. "Not yet."

Breanna nodded, satisfied. Hazel looked her in the eye.

"Okay," Breanna replied.

She took a slow, shaky breath that her nonphysical body didn't need, and then let it out. She shut her eyes. Hazel breathed with her. The minutes dragged on, the other girls still grouped around them like a tense security team, waiting.

After a few more breaths, Breanna stopped shaking and her face looked serene. When she finally smiled, her shoulders dropped as if the tension had left her, and she faded away.

Hazel stayed where she knelt a moment longer, feeling Breanna's absence like a light had burned out. First went Gran, then probably her mom, then Breanna, and before too long it would be Kelly; Hazel felt the loneliness in her stomach. She heaved a heavy sigh, thinking it would at least be easy to let go when her time came. She dragged herself up and faced the others.

"Breanna's gone," she said, her own shoulders slumping with exhaustion. "She said to say goodbye to you."

Morgan pinched her lower lip with her fingers. Riva wrapped Hazel in a hug, forcing her to scrunch up her nose to fight back a sob. She looked up at the disappearing stars as the sky turned pink. No birds sang to welcome the dawn.

"And Kelly?" Riva asked when they broke apart.

"I don't know. I haven't seen her since last night," Hazel said, dabbing at her nose.

Riva read her expression. "Don't worry. She'll be back."

"The lavender," Hazel reminded her, and she couldn't keep the despair out of her voice.

"Even so," Riva said.

Hazel dug the lavender from her backpack. Weighing it in her hands, she turned to the others and said, "We light this, and fill the house with smoke. Start at the bottom of the walls, and waft it into every crack, moving up. We should leave a door or window open for the smoke to get out after. But what's really important is our intentions. You have to concentrate on demanding that any negativity leave; that the shadow isn't welcome here anymore. And it's not allowed to hurt any of us.

Be firm on that. But be grateful at the same time."

"Grateful to the shadow?" Di asked, surprised.

"No... More like, grateful for the lavender. You have to feel positive and peaceful."

The girls were looking awkward as Hazel passed out the lavender.

"Don't worry, you'll get it once we get started."

"And the shadow will just leave?" Riva asked, rolling the stems of her bundle between her fingers.

Hazel looked at the house. They had left the front door ajar in their hurry to get away, making it look more abandoned than any other house in the neighbourhood.

"Let's go," she said, choosing not to answer. She lit the end of her lavender.

Come In

Shielding the little flame with her hand, Hazel crossed the lawn. The dog barked and resisted Di's lead, digging in its paws. The cat hissed.

"I'll put them in the backyard," Di whispered, and she disappeared around the side of the house. The cat streaked after her, determined not to be left behind.

Hazel climbed the front steps. Her pulse sped up with every step closer, like she was pressing on a gas pedal that revved her own heart. The darkness within the small crack of the open door was alive with imagined movement. Too afraid of what might happen if she stretched out her hand for the doorknob, Hazel nudged the door open with her foot. She paused on the threshold to allow her eyes to adjust.

"Here," Jen said from the bottom of the steps, and she passed Hazel a flashlight.

With the lavender in her left hand and the light in her right, Hazel stepped inside. She opened her heart, and directed her silent 'leave' message to the shadow. She nodded at Jen, who had followed her inside. Setting the flashlight down on the coffee table, Hazel went to the window, wafting the lavender from floor to ceiling with her hand. Jen imitated her, moving down the hallway to the first bedroom. So far so good.

Riva tackled the kitchen, and Alexis the bathroom. Without complaint, Morgan crossed the hallway beam over the open basement to reach the master bedroom. Riva stalled in the kitchen as Hazel came closer and closer to the basement door. Everyone was avoiding downstairs. Hazel's palm was sweaty against the lavender stems and she wished someone else would volunteer. She paused with her arm raised, smoke curling from the smoldering lavender. Hazel could feel her heart-rate quickening already.

"There's another body out there," Di said, shutting the front door behind her. Hazel dropped her lavender in fright.

"You scared me," she gasped, scooping the smoking bundle back up and refusing to turn her back on the basement.

"Sorry. What do you think it means?"

Hazel continued contemplating the glass doorknob as Jen arrived behind her.

"I saw the first body after the shadow attacked Riva," Hazel said, "which it had never done before. If there's another body now...maybe it can attack again."

"You think the corrupt are the shadow's food? Like we are theirs?"

"Ugh, please don't put it like that," Jen said, with a shiver.

Hazel stopped listening as she wafted the smoke over the door, taking a step closer.

"Do you want help down there?" Di asked, seeing Hazel was not to be distracted.

Hazel hesitated. She was scared, but she didn't want to be responsible for putting Di in danger.

"I missed out on doing up here. I drew the short straw," Di said, lighting her handful of lavender. "We'll go together."

"Me too," Jen said, grabbing the flashlight. The beam

trembled in her hand.

Hazel felt a surge of gratitude even as her heart tried to beat its way out of her body and away from the shadow.

"I'll go first," she said, sounding hoarse.

She used her toe to thrust the door open again.

From the depths of the basement, the half-male, half-female shadow sang, "Come in!"

Hazel's hair prickled up as she stared into the darkness for the source of the voice.

"Don't go," Di squeaked, taking it all back. She grabbed Hazel's arm.

"We have to do it, one way or the other," Hazel whispered. She couldn't make her voice come out any stronger.

She sent the lavender in first, obscuring her view even more.

She cleared her throat and called to the shadow, "I've hated you since I was six years old. Leave! You aren't welcome here, and you are not allowed to harm us, anymore. This is not your house, and it's time to get out."

There was no response. Hazel shifted to the left so Jen could shine the flashlight on the stairs. It was a small comfort that there was no way for reaching hands to grab her through the steps until the bottom. She took a steadying breath and descended the stairs, Jen and Di at her heels. She sent the smoke from steps to ceiling as she walked. The wooden floorboards creaked as she passed over them.

Heart hammering again, she reached the final open-backed stairs. She moved neither faster nor slower despite visions of horror movies and hands grabbing ankles. She didn't want to give the shadow the satisfaction of knowing she was afraid. Her feet landed on the cement, and Jen raised the flashlight behind her so she could see into the corners of the room. The light couldn't reach that far.

Nothing but a gut feeling made Hazel suspect the corner furthest from the front windows, under the ripped up hallway. The missing floor left a gaping hole in the ceiling, but still no light came in. She stepped to the wall and continued the familiar process of cleansing from floor to ceiling. Then Jen yelped and Hazel and Di whipped around.

"What is it?" Hazel asked, rushing to her side.

"It said my name," Jen said, her free hand clamped over her left ear as she stared into the same dark corner, shaking.

Hazel bluffed for Jen's sake. "That's not so bad. It's just words. Sticks and stones, right? Try and ignore it. We're almost rid of it. Come on, keep going."

She went back to work right away, Jen still breathing hard where she stood. Hazel knew how horrifying that voice was, but they had to get on with the job.

As she made another motion from floor to ceiling, Hazel thought she heard a small shuffling sound from the hallway corner. Her eyes adjusting to the dark, she saw shelves running up the far wall, with a long wooden tabletop built in at hip-height. On the table was the collection of tools they had been borrowing to seal up the house. She thought she could make out the curve of a table-saw and an open chest of tools.

"What are you looking at?" Di demanded, catching her at it.

"The tools," Hazel said. "We might want them upstairs at some point."

"Where is...it?" Di asked. "Is the smoke working?"

"I'm sure it is," Hazel lied. "Why don't you do the back of the stairs? We don't want to miss a single crack."

A thump came from the darkest corner. Hazel whirled around to see the cord of the power saw dangling over the edge of the table, swinging. She sped up her cleansing of the wall, floor to ceiling, floor to ceiling. She tried to focus, but couldn't quell the sensation of someone standing over her shoulder. She looked back. The dark bulged forwards, like a light overhead had gone out.

"Hazel..." Jen said, who was staring in the same direction. "Do you see something over there that I don't?"

"No, just shadow," but even as she said it, Hazel saw the outline of a black figure.

Its face was bowed and hidden by the gloom. The over-long limbs were frozen at its sides. The longer she stared at it and nothing happened, the faster Hazel breathed.

It was one of the hardest things Hazel ever had to do, turning back to the wall. She started counting her breaths in her head, elongating them as much as she could. She passed under the boarded windows and shivered. A drip of nervous sweat tickled her eyebrow. There was an exhale on her neck. Or perhaps she had imagined it. Her eyes passed over the cracks in the cement wall, the only things she allowed herself to look at besides the rising and falling of her hand holding the lavender.

"You aren't welcome here," she muttered to the shadow again. "Leave now. This is not your house. You are not allowed to hurt us."

Hazel was so aware of the figure in the corner she might as well have had eyes on the back of her head. The closer she got to it, the more her skin prickled and cried out for her to run. She found the table that ran along the back wall. She turned to the shelves, ready to cleanse them with smoke, and let her eyes flash to the corner. The figure was still standing there. Hazel almost wished it would move. She wondered if it was watching her out of the corner of its eye now. Its head had not even tilted.

There was movement to the right. Di was headed towards the figure with her lavender, much closer than Hazel had guessed.

"Di—"

The figure turned, stiff as a statue, in Di's direction. Hazel's lungs stopped working. She dropped her lavender.

"Di, run!" she gasped, breathless.

Instinct made Di turn to the shadow instead. It flashed towards her, flickering like a strobe light between lunges so that Hazel never saw its feet move. It was on Di before Hazel had set down her first step.

In one vicious downwards swipe, the shadow scratched Di's eyes with both hands. Di screamed and fell to her knees, clutching at her face. Red blood poured from her empty eye sockets. There was a thunderous sound overhead. It was like the dream where Hazel's feet were stuck to the pavement again; every action slower than life, the weight of her feet too much to lift.

The shadow turned its face to Hazel and she saw its true form for the first time, no darkness, just Kelly's blood-stained cheeks, red from the human flesh her teeth had torn into. She saw Kelly's blue eyes clouded over like curdled milk; Kelly's purple veins standing out against her pale skin, the blood solid and no longer pumping. Her clothes were still torn and stained where the zombies at school had ripped into her lower back. Her hair was matted and stiffened with blood. She sneered at Hazel, dropped to her knees over Di, and opened her mouth wide. She closed her lips over Di's eye and made a sucking sound that Di's rattling, high-pitched scream couldn't overpower as she thrashed on the floor.

Hazel realized she was screaming too. Her legs gave way as she stopped trying to pull them from the quicksand-like cement. She saw Jen bearing down on her. Riva was leaping down the last stairs with Morgan and Alexis right behind her. They all flickered the way the shadow had, as if her brain couldn't take in any more horror and would only let her see a flash at a time. She couldn't stop screaming long enough to warn the girls away. Her throat went raw in seconds.

"Di!" she screamed, pointing at her. The words came with difficulty. "SAVE HER!"

Instead, firm hands grabbed her arms, and Hazel dissolved into a fit of screams as she was dragged towards the shadow. In a flash, Kelly was digging her hands into Jen. Flash—her teeth tore at Riva. Flash—now Alexis, now Morgan.

"Cover her mouth," someone said. "I can't take it anymore!"

Hazel once again had the bizarre experience of opening eyes she had thought were already open. She snapped her mouth shut, and the screaming coming from it stopped. The screaming coming from Di went on. Hazel jerked into a sitting position, causing a few more shouts of alarm.

She was sitting on the kitchen floor in the dark, facing the basement door. All the remaining furniture in the house had been pushed up against it. She heard a slap, and Di's scream stopped for a millisecond.

"Pour some water on her!" came another voice.

Hazel's eyes darted around so fast she could see colours swimming behind every blurry object and person. Di was lying next to her.

"Hazel," the blur in front of her said. "Can you see me?"

"You're blurry," Hazel croaked. "Oh god, why can't I see you?"

"Calm down," came Riva's voice. "Calm down. I've got you."

She felt something brush her arm and flinched.

"It's just me," Riva said, and Hazel could hear the worry in her voice.

Her face came into focus.

"What happened to Di?" Hazel demanded.

Riva tried to soothe her. "She's right here. We're just trying to snap her out of it."

Water ricocheted off Di's face and splashed Hazel. At last, the screaming stopped.

Hazel crawled over to Di, and lifted a closed eyelid with her thumb. All she could see was the white of Di's eye. Hazel collapsed beside her, relief flooding her limbs with warmth. Coming into focus, Jen, Riva, Morgan, and Alexis all exchanged confused looks.

"What happened to her?" Hazel asked.

"We were hoping you could tell us that," Jen said. "You could see something we couldn't."

"I saw the shadow. But it was Kelly. She scratched Di's eyes out and then-then—," she paused to shudder and pull her words together, "drank them. From her head."

Disgusted, they all looked at Di.

"But it wasn't really Kelly, was it?" Alexis said at the same time as Riva asked, "But she's fine, right?"

"I don't know. And the shadow was probably just messing with me, with a vision of Kelly. But I don't know. It's a... It's a hard vision to shake. We have to get out of here. The furniture won't keep the shadow away from us."

"But the lavender—"

"It didn't work downstairs."

"But we weren't finished," Jen said. "We got everywhere up here, but we didn't get through the whole basement before it... you know."

"It's not worth it," Hazel said. She realized she was sweating at the thought of staying.

"But—"

"Show her," Morgan said.

Hazel looked from one to the other. Jen got up and went to the living room, waving for Hazel to come with her. Hazel got to her feet as if she hadn't stood up in years, all her muscles aching. Jen pointed to the peephole in the door. Hazel peered through and gasped. Outside were rows of the corrupt, all staring straight at them. They were standing where the girls had stood less than half an hour ago. Hazel followed the line down both sides of the house, where it curved and continued on.

"Ohhh...that can't be good."

The First One

"We're surrounded," Jen confirmed. "We're definitely at the centre of this."

"The shadow is the centre of this..." Hazel said, her heart sinking at the memory of why the lavender was so important.

"They do seem like they're under someone's control, don't they," Jen agreed, her face grim.

"Okay. How are we going to get out of this?" Hazel muttered, rubbing her eyes.

When she looked back up, she saw that Jen was studying her.

"What?"

"I think you're amazing."

Hazel's eyebrows raised of their own accord. Her mouth opened, but nothing came out. Brave, kind, competitive, gorgeous Jen thought she, Hazel, was amazing?

"You bounce back so fast," Jen explained, her face reddening. "You're onto the next thing before the rest of us have stopped panicking."

"I have to."

Jen shook her head. "No, you don't. You are...you just..."

She waved her hands, unable to come up with the right words. She gave Hazel an apologetic smile.

"Hazel," Riva called from the kitchen, "what's your medical opinion on this? What does Di need?"

There was an embarrassed silence. Hazel's heart, so low moments before, had risen high enough to lift her chest. They shared another smile, then hurried back to the kitchen.

"I don't have a medical opinion," Hazel admitted. "It was all Kelly. But she won't be able to come in here now. Because of the lavender."

Riva looked disappointed. Hazel's lifted heart slumped back down again.

There was barking from the back door and Morgan stood up to check on the dog. "He's barking at the house. And the cat's hiding in the bushes, I can see its eyes reflecting."

Hazel said nothing. It was disturbing; the dog was more worried about the house than the zombies surrounding it.

The sun was up now, and the girls jumped at every creak and shadow as the house warmed up. They were all exhausted from the previous day's run, but no one could sleep. They were too afraid of the zombies outside, pressing up against the backyard fence, and of the shadow inside, blocked only by the lavender.

Alexis was huddled over a backpack on the fold-out couch, her eyes darting to the basement door and back. "I can't believe no one has come to help us yet."

"They still might," Riva said. "They've probably just escaped themselves, with the corrupt all frozen last night. They know what it's like to be trapped, they'll make sure we get help. Anyway, the corrupt all surrounding us has got to look suspicious. It's only a matter of time before someone comes."

"It's only a matter of time until we're attacked by them. Or 'it,'" Alexis said. "They better get here sooner than later."

"Won't matter," Morgan said, playing with the sling around

her neck, "according to Hazel."

Hazel put down the lighter she was fiddling with. "Still, I'd like to get out of here."

There was a huge gasp. Hazel dropped her lighter and leapt to her feet. Alexis fumbled the backpack. Riva and Morgan grabbed their spears and whipped around, looking for an attacker.

"I'm blind!" Di screamed on the bed beside Alexis. "Oh god, I'm blind!"

Alexis did the only thing she could, and grabbed Di's hand. Di screamed again and tried to pull away.

"It's just me, it's just me!" Alexis cried, hands raised in a supplicating gesture that Di couldn't see.

Di struggled against the sheets they had tucked over her, fighting to get up. Riva pushed her back down, but this was a mistake. Di freaked out worse than ever and struck Riva across the face. She fell back, clutching her nose. Hazel clambered over Alexis and squashed Di in a tight hug before she could lash out again.

"It's me, it's Hazel, you're okay, you're okay."

Hazel had a deja-vu of herself under the covers, soothing Kelly as the shadow loomed over them both.

"Hazel, my eyes!"

Di's eyes were blank and darting. Her short hair was a mess of white tendrils around her face. Hazel took Di's hand and pressed it over her eyelid.

"You still have your eyes," she said. "Can you feel them under your palm?"

"Y-yes," Di choked.

Hazel let go so she could feel both eyes with her hands.

"But I can't see!" Di sobbed.

"It will probably wear off," Hazel said with an attempt at confidence. "The welt on Riva's arm is healing."

"That's true," Riva said, raising her arm to show Di where the shadow had grabbed her. She dropped it again when Di stared hopelessly in her direction.

"What if it doesn't?"

"It will," Hazel said.

Still reeling, Di asked, "Where are we?"

"In the living room."

"We're still here?" Di shrieked.

"Nothing has happened for hours," Alexis reassured her.

Di opened her mouth to protest, but Hazel interrupted to tell her about being surrounded. To her surprise, the next question out of Di's mouth was, "What about the dog and cat?"

"They're outside. We fed them."

"Are they safe out there?"

"The corrupt aren't moving, just like last night."

"What if they attack?"

It was the question they had all been asking themselves.

"They won't come inside anyways," Jen said. "The animals. I tried."

"Doesn't that say something?" Di asked. "Why don't we try just...walking past the corrupt?"

"Don't do that," Kelly said.

Hazel wheeled around on the sheets so fast they twisted with her and she cricked her neck.

"What is it?" Riva asked, clutching her spear again.

"What—how are you here?" Hazel spluttered.

"I can smell the lavender," Kelly said, nodding. "I don't know. But no one else can get in."

"What do you mean? Who else?"

"Other people who got killed. Not that they really want in. But they tried so they could warn you. I'm the only one who made it."

"That doesn't make sense."

"Hazel, what's going on?" Di asked.

"Kelly got in."

"Is it really Kelly?" Di asked, her voice high-pitched as she clutched the sheets, terrified.

Hazel considered her sister. Her eyes were the dark blue Hazel knew, her skin unblemished and clean, and her hair in chestnut waves.

"Why are you looking at me like that?" Kelly asked.

There was no way to tell, and the longer she stared, the more Hazel's skin crawled.

Di's voice was pleading. "Hazel?"

"Ghosts can't get in," Hazel whispered.

Di drew in her feet and whimpered, reaching out to grab Alexis. They slid off the mattress in each other's arms. The group faced the supposed ghost with Hazel in the forefront. She got up to stand between the others and the shadow, bracing for an attack.

"What do you want?" she asked, fists clenched.

Offended, Kelly's mouth hung open. "To give you the news. What's wrong with all of you?"

Hazel waited.

Kelly frowned and said, "There are ghosts out there watching what's going on. I spoke to some of the nurses from the hospital. Mom's ward. They said... They said the first one was Gran."

"Gran?" Hazel asked in spite of herself.

"When she died they let Mom have a moment with her, and then th-they heard sc-screaming." Kelly choked back a sob.

"Gran came back to life and they saw her r-rip Mom's throat open."

Hazel felt like she was falling into the basement. "That's not true."

"Stop listening to it, Hazel!" Di said. "Please, let's get out of here!"

Kelly looked hurt. Tears fell as she whispered, "I saw her, Hazel. I saw Gran. The nurses took me to see her. She's one of them. She's still in her n-nightgown."

"She wasn't attacked," Hazel argued. "She can't be one of them."

"I saw her," Kelly persisted. "She didn't need to be killed that way. She started everything."

"You started everything!" Hazel yelled.

"What are you talking about?" Kelly asked in apparent frustration.

"Grab some lavender," Hazel said over her shoulder.

Jen dove at a bundle that was still sitting on the side-table. Riva snatched up the lighter and they lit it together. Then Jen rushed to Hazel's side and waved it in the air between her and Kelly.

"It doesn't work, remember?" Kelly said, watching the waving lavender under her nose with a wounded frown.

"Yes, it does!" cried a voice down the hallway.

All seven of them turned towards the voice.

"Hazel, run!" it called in Kelly's frightened voice. "Get away from it!"

"Who-who is that?" asked the Kelly in the living room.

"We didn't smoke the corner of the basement," Jen said. "Kelly can still get in there. Her voice is coming up through the hole!"

"Come here!" the voice from the hallway screamed.

The furniture around the basement door rattled. Pieces fell away. The microwave on the top of the pile crashed to the ground and burst apart, forcing Riva further into the living room. They looked to the hallway, the only other way to the basement, but the Kelly in the living room was still blocking their way.

Alexis gasped. Even without seeing the shadow, she understood what was happening. "We're trapped!"

A lamp near the window fell over and the lightbulb shattered at Morgan's feet. Morgan jumped aside and raised her spear like a club in her good hand. Teeth clenched, she charged, parted the girls, and took a chance swing at Kelly.

"Morgan, no!" Hazel cried, grabbing her shoulder.

The spear passed straight through Kelly, and she only flinched. Morgan shook Hazel off and ran down the hallway with a cry of victory. The other girls followed, Di clinging to Alexis for guidance. Hazel remained where she stood, sensing that something was wrong. The Kelly in the basement yesterday had been dead-eyed and bloody. This Kelly was normal-looking and afraid.

"Wait!" Hazel cried, chasing after the girls.

The hallway erupted in screams. Fearing the worst, Hazel broke into the group at the corner. The Kelly from the living room followed at her heels. There, the decaying Kelly Hazel had seen in the basement was clinging to Morgan's legs as it dragged her over the ledge. Its roving fingernails left bloody scratches down Morgan's back. Jen and Riva tugged at her arms as she shrieked in pain.

"Help me!" Morgan screamed, her eyes wide with terror.

Hazel dove at the edge and grabbed Morgan's sling at her

neck. Morgan screamed in more pain, but bent over the fabric so that Hazel was hoisting her from around the ribs. With Riva and Jen's help, they pulled Morgan up so that only her legs were over the gap. Kelly's torso lifted out of the basement with her. It cackled as it tried to claw Morgan back down. Jen kicked at its face, but its head barely jerked back. It hissed and fixed its eyes on her. It seemed to be becoming more solid, more visible.

"Get off her!" Kelly roared from beside Hazel.

It fixed its eyes on Kelly.

"Come to the basement," it said, back in its own dual voice. It slithered off of Morgan and disappeared into the darkness.

Retreat

They moved outside and didn't waste a minute before barricading the backyard. All that day they sweat in the summer heat, taking down the boards in the house and moving them to the tiny shed. Moving as fast as they could, the girls ripped a mattress and their supplies out of the house and filled the shed's floor so that there was no walking room. They would have to sleep with their backs against the walls.

"It's just until rescue comes," Alexis reminded them, a nail between her teeth as she worked.

Hazel stared into the eyes of a corrupt woman with long, curly hair as she reinforced the fence between them. The woman stared back, watchful, but frozen. Hazel frowned at her. Why had the shadow chased them out of the house, only to trap them there again? The dog, who they named Rescue, barked behind Hazel. She turned to see Jen going up the back steps. Rescue barked every time someone went inside. Meanwhile, Di sat in the grass with the cat, stroking its fur and waiting for the dog to return the stick she had tossed. They called the cat Di's Buddy because it never left her side. It kept its yellow eyes on the corrupt, as if aware that Di couldn't see them.

"Why doesn't the thing attack us now?" Morgan wanted to know as she passed Riva nails. The scratches on her back bled if she moved too much.

"I think I know," Kelly said.

"Kelly knows, apparently," Hazel told her, wandering over. To Kelly she said, "You know that, but you don't know how you got past the lavender?"

Kelly's brow creased with hurt. "I'm your sister. Maybe I'm special too."

Riva was hammering a makeshift catch to the inside of the shed's door frame so they could slip a bar of wood across the door if need be. Hazel watched her and wondered.

"The nurses told me they saw the shadow when it got mom," Kelly went on. "It got visible right as she died, then faded again."

"It's like it gets power from death," Hazel said, trying to ignore the comment about their mother. "That's what I thought too."

"It's not just that. When Gran died, no one saw the shadow. I think Gran was too tired to be afraid. But with Mom... The more fear, the more...juice."

"That does explain the visions. It uses them to terrify its victims before they die so it gets more out of them."

"What explains the visions?" Morgan asked, annoyed.

Hazel passed on Kelly's intel.

"So," Kelly said, "it also seems to need to recharge between attacks. But the thing is..."

"What?"

"Why did it want to kill you? If you have an endless supply of people to traumatize and reap fear from, why does it need to kill at all? Why does it need to kill its own zombies?"

"Why does it need to kill its own zombies..." Hazel repeated.

"They're doing the dirty work," Morgan said, jumping in as

best she could with only half the conversation. "They collect the fear. The thing collects from them."

"Huh," Hazel said, intrigued. "That boy-zombie on the lawn showed up right before the shadow attacked Riva. Maybe he make it strong enough to attack her. Maybe the official, final kill gives it the biggest boost. It's like a bit of fear is a taste, but a human kill is like a bite, and a corrupt kill is a meal because it gets all the fear from all the humans that that corrupt killed."

Morgan shrugged. "I wish we couldn't smell it."

The day went on with no sighting of the shadow, even with the girls going in and out through the unblocked back door. They always went in pairs, just in case. When evening fell, Hazel was confident that the shed could withstand an attack. Di was more anxious.

"There's so many of them, if they all attack us they could knock the shed right over," she worried.

"Most of them won't know we're in here," Jen said, settling down cross-legged on the mattress beside a large pile of extra lumber. "They can't see us over the house."

"The shadow could tell them."

Jen hadn't thought of that. "I don't know, it's pretty secure."

It was true. Gran liked to garden before she got sick, and had invested in a decent little building. It was blue on the outside and had a sloped ceiling like a miniature house with no windows. The girls had succeeded in reinforcing the walls on the inside. They used the ejected gardening equipment as spikes around the fence, or left them out as convenient weapons to grab.

They settled under their blankets, exhausted and sore, with more than one hammered thumb. Jen, Morgan, and Riva sat opposite Hazel and Di. Morgan's feet kept touching Hazel's, which neither of them liked. Kelly sat with her legs across them all, but no one could tell.

"I really need a shower," sighed Riva, wafting her pajama top.

There were mumbles of agreement all around.

"How are your eyes, Di?" Jen asked. "Any change?"

Di shook her head. "I don't know if I should leave them open or closed."

No one knew what to say that, so they all made sympathetic noises instead.

"Hazel?" Di asked. "Did Kelly say anything else? Besides all that stuff about fear? Does she know how to get rid of the corrupt?"

"No," Hazel said.

She had been trying to avoid the rest of Kelly's announcements all day. Her face grew hot and Riva threw her a look.

"I think we all need to know everything," she coaxed.

Hazel looked at Kelly, whose eyes were fixed on her feet.

"She said my gran started it. The shadow corrupted her and she turned into the first zombie. And the first person Gran killed was my mom." She spoke in a dispassionate monotone, but her eyes filled with tears that fell of their own accord. She gasped for air as she went on, "I can't stop thinking about h-how my mom must have felt. She loved Gran so much. She didn't deserve this. And now I'll n-never get to see her again!"

Hazel buried her face in her hands as both Riva and Di lunged across the mattress to hug her.

"My wh-whole family..." Hazel sobbed into the group hug, wanting more than anything to grab Kelly's hand for comfort.

"No, not your whole family," Riva reminded her, squeezing her tight.

"But where will I go after this?" Hazel asked. "How can I live without…"

Di was crying too. "Things are going to be different," she said. "For all of us. But if we're alive, even if that's all we've got, that's what we hang onto."

Hazel grieved everything she had been holding in since the attacks started onto Riva's shoulder. She felt a great gap down her chest, like her whole sternum was missing. She collapsed around that aching gash to keep herself together. Once, her eyes fell on Alexis, who was staring at the opposite wall like it might offer her comfort. She remembered what Breanna told her about Alexis' aunt. Alexis only had her brother left too, but Hazel couldn't bring herself to make Alexis feel the way she did. It was too terrible. Instead, she felt the extra pain for her.

"Hazel," Kelly said after a time, with a hitch mid-word, "I'm still here too. And I'm not going anywhere. Wherever you go, I'll go."

Hazel's chest ached worse than ever, but she couldn't argue. As the other girls fell asleep, Riva stayed awake into the night, never letting her go.

The morning sun dragged itself across the sky, and the shed grew scorching hot and stuffy. Morgan crawled one-armed across the dozing bodies to pull the boards from the door and squeeze out the crack with the dog. Hazel felt the fresh air on her face and couldn't stay inside any longer. She crawled away from Riva, who had passed out with her face against the wall. Hazel pulled the mattress back to get the door open further and struggled out.

The grass was a brilliant green with dew still resting on the blades. Hazel ran her hands through it and wiped her face. Morgan had disappeared around the side of the house to take a bathroom break. When she returned, she offered Hazel a roll of toilet paper.

"See anything new?" Hazel asked.

"Over the fence," Morgan nodded, pointing towards their designated outdoor toilet.

Hazel wandered over, letting the grass cool her bare feet. She skirted the fence alongside the house, eyes on the windows for any signs of life within. She stood on her toes to look out over the driveway. Craning her neck, she could see the boy's body still lying on the front grass. Next to him was a woman, face up, with blood all over her mouth and glazed eyes drying in the sun. Beside her, Hazel could just make out another foot, the attached body blocked by the house.

She took her bathroom break with many nervous glances at the house and the watching corrupt. When she returned, she saw a ladder pushed up against the shed. Morgan was surveying the zombie circle from the roof. Hazel climbed up to join her.

"Another one," Hazel said, getting her footing on the sandpaper-like shingles.

"Yep. What should we do?"

Hazel shrugged again. She felt drained, even after the night's sleep. She stared out at the corrupt crowding the fence and yawned.

Morgan gritted her teeth. "Where are the police? They've got riot gear. Where are the helicopters? They're safe up high! Where's the news? Why are we on our own?"

"I don't know."

"Well it's ridiculous!" she snapped. "I say we smoke the rest of the basement and get the hell out of here."

"How?" Hazel asked, gesturing at the corrupt. "And what about what happened to Di? It tried really hard to stop us. What if it kills us?"

"Well, send Di in," Morgan said. "She can't see anything now, so it can't scare her to death."

Hazel blinked in shock. "That's harsh."

"True though," Morgan said, folding her arms. "She's still better off than the rest of us."

"I don't call being blind better off. And it could still give her visions."

"Why does everyone argue with me?" Morgan asked, throwing up her hands. "No one else is coming up with anything proactive!"

Hazel knew Morgan wasn't serious about sending Di in. "I think the burning does need to be done eventually. And sooner than later. But we also need a break. If we don't see any signs of the shadow today, I think we deserve to recharge just as much as it does. Don't you think?"

Morgan turned away, grumpy. She was not a morning person. Hazel headed back to the ladder.

"Look," Morgan said, "I'm sorry about your family, alright? But we can't afford to grieve right now. We have to stay focused. This thing could be getting stronger."

Hazel opened her mouth in anger. Then she shut her eyes and took a calming breath. "It's not about grieving," she said, lowering her voice. "Look at Riva. She's been awake for most of two days. She won't be at her best if we don't give her some time to rest."

"She wouldn't have been up all last night if you hadn't—"

"Hadn't what?" Hazel asked, anger flaring back up again.

"I'm just saying, we don't have time for feeling sad."

"Sad? Sad? My mom, my grandmother, my sister—"

"I know, I know, and I'm really sorry for your loss and everything, but we have bigger things to worry about! And don't look at me like that, I'm not the one putting the pressure on, it's them!" she pointed in the direction of the corrupt.

"Bottle it up all you want," Hazel said, her voice cold, "but don't expect the rest of us to hide from it."

Hazel climbed down the ladder and walked away, but as space was limited, she found herself staring over the front fence at the bodies again. She picked at a scratch on her palm and wondered if she or Morgan was stronger.

At noon, Riva came tearing out of the shed, sweating and angry.

"Why didn't anyone wake me?" she demanded.

"You needed to rest," Hazel said.

"Me?" Riva exclaimed. "What about you?"

"I couldn't sleep anymore."

"Well you should have tried. What have you been working on? Let me take over and you go have a nap. Fill me in."

"Riva, you're going to wear yourself out," Hazel said. "Relax a little. We've just been adding to the fence a bit and thinking about how to get past the corrupt. We're not rushing around like the last two days. Nothing's happening. It's quiet. You can think about yourself for once."

Riva looked like she didn't know how. Her glance darted from Hazel, who was sitting in the shade of the back fence, to Di, Jen and Alexis, who were all petting the animals. All four girls were sitting in a curved line with Kelly at the end, though they couldn't see her. Morgan was still on the roof of the shed.

"Seriously," Hazel said, tossing Riva a can of peaches, "we're just thinking things through. Come and sit down."

Reluctant as she was, Riva sat down with the others, her back to the house. It was obvious from her frequent shoulder checks that she didn't like it.

"How are you?" she asked Hazel.

"I'm fine," Hazel said. When Riva looked disbelieving, she added, "Really. I feel better now."

The ache in her chest wasn't as bad today. She knew she could call up her grief faster than she could breathe, but succumbing to it last night had made it easier to keep at bay.

"We were just talking about fire," Jen said. "We haven't used that on the zombies yet."

"They wouldn't feel it," Riva said.

"That's what Hazel was saying. But I think if it breaks them down, they can't attack anymore. I think it's the only way to destroy them."

Riva looked uneasy. Hazel pictured flaming zombies chasing them down.

"We saw some helicopters out that way," Alexis said, pointing into the distance behind the house. "I think they're making their way over here. It must be easier to get people out with the zombies out of the way. I bet they'll get here within the day."

Riva sat up straighter. "Are you serious? We might be rescued today?"

Alexis' smile twitched. "Try not to get your hopes up."

"Then we can tell them to try fire when they get here," Jen added.

"And that's why we should get rid of this shadow now," Morgan called from the top of the shed. "They're not just going to let us stay here to take care of it whenever we feel like. They'll make us evacuate."

"I think we're stuck anyway. What are they going to do if the corrupt attack when they try to get past them?"

"Helicopters go up," Morgan said.

There was a moment of silence, then Jen snorted and the

other girls grinned.

Fatality

"**H**eads up!" Morgan cried, clattering and sliding down the ladder. "Grab your weapons!"

The girls had been brainstorming in the middle of the yard and had their weapons at their sides. Even so, Morgan went tearing down the side of the house before anyone had time for questions. Hazel could feel her pulse pounding in her throat as she gripped her homemade spear.

"What's going on?" Alexis' voice called from the outdoor toilet on the other side of the house.

Hazel caught up to Morgan looking out over the front lawn. Her grip on her weapon had gone slack. Hazel followed her gaze, but the smell preceded the source. Three fresh bodies were on the lawn. Hazel raised her shirt to cover her nose.

"Think they saw me and dropped dead of fright?" Morgan asked as Riva, Jen, and Kelly joined them.

Hazel gave a reluctant grin. She felt chilled despite the sun blazing on her neck.

"Where's Di and Alexis?" Kelly asked, noticing they were two girls short.

Hazel left the stench behind to check on the girls. The shed door was shut, so she knocked there first.

"It's Hazel, are you in there?"

The door flew open to reveal a frightened Di.

"You all left, and I couldn't see where you were going," she sobbed. She was clutching the end of Rescue's leash like she was terrified of separation from him.

"Oh god, I'm so sorry," Hazel gasped, taking Di's shaking hands so she could tell where Hazel was. "I thought someone else had you." She looked over Di's shoulder at the empty mattresses. "Where's Alexis?"

"She-she's not with you?"

Hazel glanced back at the other girls, who shook their heads that Alexis was not with them.

"I'll check the 'bathroom,'" Riva said, running off and calling Alexis' name.

Jen's eyes went wide. "She didn't think we went inside, did she?"

Morgan and Hazel both spun around to look at the house.

"She's not here!" Riva called.

Morgan and Hazel exchanged a look and bolted to the back door together, leaving Jen to take care of Di. They dropped their weapons and grabbed lavender and the lighter on the way. Hazel wrenched the backdoor open and crossed the threshold, calling for Alexis. There was no answer as she cranked the lighter, which sputtered twice before starting. She ran to check the bathroom, hoping Alexis was there.

"The basement door is still shut," Morgan said, not slowing as she raced down the hallway to the bedrooms.

"Alexis," Hazel sighed when she opened the bathroom door. She clutched her heart with relief. "Why did you come in here by yourself?"

She realized Alexis was sobbing.

"Are you alright?"

Alexis turned away, her face buried in her hands. She was too distraught to speak.

"What is it?" Hazel asked, worried.

She raised a hand to touch Alexis' shoulder, but her hand met no fabric or skin. It sank like Hazel was wafting air. Her mouth fell open as Morgan ran passed again, noticing nothing.

"No!"

"It showed me what it did to my aunt," Alexis sobbed, "It showed me what it did to her-to her—soul."

"What did it do?" Hazel whispered, her limbs numb with the shock.

Alexis sank to her knees and curled in on herself. "It ate it."

It was a long moment before Hazel could speak. She struggled to pull air into her lungs. "How did it... How did it get you?"

Alexis sobbed harder than ever and rocked where she sat. She looked as alive as she had moments before. The difference was that she seemed to be sliding towards the outside wall. The smoke was doing its job and banishing her from the house.

"I thought you all went in the house, but when I came in, it c-came out of the b-basement," she moaned. "It was stronger than the lavender."

"It just fed on three corrupt," Hazel said.

"I tried to get away," Alexis said, "before it could get my soul too. But it only stopped when it heard you."

Hazel didn't need to hear more. The shadow was lying in wait, and she and Morgan were in the house with it. She turned on her heel and dashed back to the living room, the bathroom door banging against the wall in her rush. Riva and Jen had just arrived in the kitchen to see if everything was okay. It took Hazel a moment to spot Morgan, who was on her knees and leaning into the corner of the living room where the lamp had broken. She was choking.

Hazel leapt over the debris in the room, grabbed Morgan by the shoulder and yanked her backwards. She fell to the floor, gasping for air. Alexis' body was crouched in the corner she had backed into before her death. One hand was still raised, bloody at the nails from Morgan's throat.

Hazel seized Morgan under her good arm and hauled her backwards. She twisted around as Hazel dragged her out the back door and down the steps, Jen and Riva at their heels. Hazel released Morgan and made a beeline for the discarded weapons. She threw one to Riva, who caught it and spun back to face the house.

"What's going on?" Riva screamed.

Crashes came from inside as Alexis' body clambered out of the corner and crossed the living room. Morgan snatched up a weapon, her injured hand stemming the flow of blood from her throat.

"Alexis?" Riva cried as the girl appeared in the doorway.

"It's not Alexis!" Hazel screamed. "Take out its eyes!"

"Hazel, what's happening?" came Di's panicked voice behind her.

"Di, get in the shed, now!"

Di scooped up the cat, and led the dog back into the shed by the leash. Alexis launched herself down the steps at Riva, then screamed in pain as Riva's knife sliced through her stomach. Hazel had forgotten the corrupt could feel pain at first. Morgan and Hazel pulled the body off Riva by Alexis' clothes, but it struggled so hard they couldn't hang onto it. Riva shook with her terror-vision.

"Eyes, Morgan, quick!" Hazel cried, trying to lock Alexis' arms behind her back. The second she touched skin, Hazel's eyes blurred with a vision of her own. She fought to keep her eyes clear as she watched the shadow cornering her.

Through the vision, she saw Jen came to their aid, freeing Morgan to strike. Morgan raised her spear, but hesitated in the face of stabbing a friend. It was Riva who tugged her knife out of Alexis' body with trembling hands and stabbed straight into her left eye. She stabbed the second eye, screaming all the while with the horror of it. They all jumped out of the newly corrupt's reach.

Di was struggling to find the shed. Hazel ran to guide her, shushing her when she gasped at the touch to her arm. There was a crash against the fence ahead. Hazel gasped. The shadow had at last released the circle of corrupt. Hazel pushed Di through the door of the shed, but Rescue broke free. His hackles were raised as he tried to defend them, growling, from the zombies.

"Don't be a hero!" she pleaded with him as the other girls dove for shelter with Di.

The first zombie cleared the fence.

"Hazel, quick!" Riva cried, holding the door open just like she had in the French room.

Hazel managed to chase the dog inside, but the zombie was within reach of her. At the same time, Alexis' body made for Riva, led by the sound of her voice. There wasn't even time for the two girls to make eye contact. Riva slammed the door. Hazel ran for the only shelter left: the house.

Let Me In

Hazel slammed and locked the back door. Thuds sounded on the other side. Her eyes darted around the room, well aware that the windows were no longer boarded. A wasp buzzed past her ear. The outside air was making its way in through the broken living room window. She didn't dare go into the basement. If she wanted to hide in the master bedroom, she would have to cross the beam over it. Her only options were the spare bedroom, or the bathroom.

Hazel snatched up a splinter of wood left over from the de-fortifying to use as a weapon. It was the size of an average knife, and thicker at the bottom. She raced to the bedroom and shut the door behind her. There was no lock.

"You'll have to get creative."

Hazel jumped and whirled around.

"What can you use?" Kelly asked.

Hazel studied her for a brief second, making sure she was the Kelly Hazel grew up with. She was clear-skinned and clean, but it was the concern in her eyes that sold it. Satisfied, Hazel yanked Jen's remaining dresser drawer out from under a pile of clothes. She stood in the middle of the room, breathing fast and holding the drawer like a shield, with no clue how to use it.

"Can you wedge the door shut?" Kelly asked. "Maybe with

pieces of it?"

Hazel smashed the drawer to the ground, aiming for the corner to hit the floor first. It burst apart and she had to cover her face to avoid the shrapnel.

"I'll be locking myself in," Hazel said aloud.

"There's always the attic."

"The corrupt can get in there. And we boarded it up, remember?"

At that moment growling came from the living room. Hazel grabbed pieces of the drawer and wedged them under the door. Her hands were fumbling. She hammered the pieces in place with the sturdiest chunk of drawer.

"Move the dresser in front of it too," Kelly said.

Hazel obeyed, feeling like her own brain wasn't working. The skeleton of the dresser scraped the hardwood floor. Pounding started on the door. She had been making too much noise to go unnoticed. Hazel threw open the closet and saw the clothes bar. She jerked it off the wall and tipped it sideways so that the clothes that hadn't been knocked down already slid into a pile.

"What are you going to do with that?" Kelly asked, reminding Hazel that most of the corrupt were beyond pain.

"I don't know!" Hazel cried in panic, dumping it back onto the floor and running her hands through her sweaty hair.

She ran to the window and pulled back the curtains. The eyes of her driving instructor looked back at her from below as he jumped to beat at the window with his fist. Feeling sick, Hazel sank to the floor where the bed used to be, drawing the bar back to her chest. She wasn't cold, but her teeth chattered. Her eyes drifted around the room. With a lurch, she saw the shadow grinning at her from the mirror.

"WHAT?" she screamed at it, her throat burning raw.

The shadow disappeared, yet Hazel's heart sank. Smoke or no, the shadow could still visit a room through the mirrors. She felt like spiders were crawling on her skin. Had the shadow been watching them all along? She grabbed some of Jen's clothes and hung them over the mirror, tucking them in behind so they would stay put. She jumped at the movements of her own reflection.

The corrupt in the attic had located the source of all the noise, or perhaps the shadow had enlightened them. They jumped up and down on the boards the girls had nailed to the attic entrance. The sound was unbelievable. Still, Hazel could hear the screaming from the backyard.

"This is it, isn't it?" she whispered.

"Someone could still come. They have the right address," Kelly said, but her tone was desperate.

Hazel shook her head. If someone was coming, they only had seconds.

"You need a-a backup plan," Kelly said. Her face full of anguish. "You don't want them killing you."

Hazel raised her hands and eyebrows in a sarcastic 'obviously' gesture.

"That's not what I mean," Kelly said, and her eyes darkened to navy with tears.

Hazel stared until something clicked.

"How would you do it?" she whispered, her lips numb.

"I see only one way that's fast enough. Th-the wood stake. Straight to the eye. You'd have to use a lot of force to drive it deep enough."

Goosebumps erupted up and down Hazel's arms, and her stomach turned over.

"I can't do that."

Kelly tried to take her hand, but swept through it. "They killed me. There's the pain, but when they touch you there's also the terror. The visions. You'll wish you'd done it."

Hazel swallowed. "What did you see? When they-when they got to you?"

Kelly hesitated. "I saw you doing it."

Hazel felt like someone had punched her in the stomach.

"Someone I trust doing that to me, not listening to my begging... It was..."

"I'm so sorry," Hazel said, tears in her eyes too.

"You didn't do anything." Kelly took a big breath and sobbed, "In fact...I think I did. I remembered something when I was being attacked. I tried to push it back down, but...it keeps coming back." She paused to collect herself. "When we were kids, I remember being so terrified one night, in this room. It was scarier than when I died."

"What happened?" Hazel asked as the window pane rattled.

"I woke up because someone was calling my name. I thought it was Gran. I heard someone say, 'Let me in, little one.' I opened the door and at the end of the hallway I saw this-this monster. I-I realize now it was me."

"I don't understand," Hazel breathed.

"I mean, when I opened the door for it I gave it permission to use me. It looked like me after this zombie attack. It was like it knew how I would die. I didn't recognize myself because I was a kid, I didn't look like that..." she trailed off.

There was a splintering sound from the hallway door. Hazel gripped the bar and the stake a little tighter.

"Then what?" she asked, trying hard to swallow. Her mouth was so dry.

"Well, I was terrified; there was a dead thing staring at me from down the hall. And you know how it feels about terror. It sort of flashed up to me and breathed me in, and down its throat I heard screaming, but my own screams weren't making any sound. It was horrible!" Kelly shivered. "Next thing I knew I was back in bed and you were saying something to me, trying to calm me down."

Hazel nodded as the door crashed against the dresser, shuddering in its frame. "I remember that night. The shadow was just standing there, staring at me."

"It wanted you," Kelly said, "but it had to settle for me. I thought it was over when I woke up beside you. But anytime I got scared after that, it would come to me in nightmares. It loved when I got scared. And remember when it stopped attacking Morgan when I yelled at it? It wasn't just out of juice. It told me to come to it. It still wants me." She looked down in shame. "All that time I thought it was just nightmares."

Kelly paused, then, with an effort, said, "And I never saw ghosts again after that."

"Saw ghosts?" Hazel asked sharply. "What do you mean?"

"The shadow fed on that part of me. I was so little at the time, I thought the weird memories I had were imaginary friends. We were so blind, thinking you were the only special one!" Kelly gasped in despair. "But it's always had its hooks in me; it's been draining me of the ability my whole life. Do you see what I'm saying now?"

Hazel shook her head as an ominous crack came from the ceiling this time.

"It needed someone that could hear it to 'open the door' for it. Someone like you and me. But in my nightmares it would show you killing me. Sometimes it was strangling, sometimes you put a pillow over my face, sometimes you pulled out my guts while I was still alive. I think it was trying to convince me to...get rid of you. But something about you made it struggle to possess you. And that same thing stopped it from coming with me when we left Gran's. It had its hook in me, but it couldn't follow the hook."

"But what was it?" Hazel asked, remembering how petrified Kelly had looked when she first saw the shadow in the basement, and how it was she who had yelled at Hazel to get the lavender. "Why you, and not me?"

"You're not afraid," Kelly said. "Not like me. It wants someone in that terrified, trance-like state where you just have to open the door to see what's out there. But you always resisted that. You kept your head."

One of the boards covering the attic came down on one side so that the nails were pointing up at the ceiling.

"I don't know about that," Hazel said, her hands sweating. "My heart feels like it's going to start smoking."

"I'm not going to leave you," Kelly promised, squaring her shoulders.

"I don't want you to see this," Hazel replied, her breath coming in short bursts.

"Haaaazzeeel..." came a voice from outside in the hallway. "Let me in..."

Hazel buried her face in her hands and whispered, "Oh my god!"

Kelly paled. "It still wants you. Even after Gran, and me, and all those others..."

There was more screaming from outside, high-pitched, followed by the barking of a dog and the yowling of a cat.

"Listen to them, Hazel," the shadow sang. "They're dying... "

Possession

"You're brave," Kelly whispered, and her distant eyes told Hazel she had thought of something. "You can make it stop. I was feeding it fear, but you don't have to. You can let it in."

Kelly turned to Hazel, tried and failed to grab her shoulders. "It's using up its energy. But if you refuse to be scared you can starve it!"

"Refuse to be scared?" Hazel repeated. She had never been more scared.

"Please!"

The 'please' stopped Hazel.

"What are you not telling me?" she asked. "Kelly, tell me!"

Kelly tensed as the window behind them cracked. "I'm here even though you cleansed this place, Hazel. I'm stuck to the shadow. I couldn't go on if I tried."

"But it can't go where there's lavender," Hazel said. "You can..."

"Because you're protecting me, the same as when we left Gran's and it couldn't follow. You have your own hooks to me. The good kind. I think you can control this shadow, Hazel."

The window shattered as Hazel stared into her sisters eyes, asking the question without words this time.

"It's always wanted you for a reason. It knows it would get power from you that it can't get from me. But maybe you can beat it."

"What if I can't?"

Kelly grimaced. "There aren't many choices."

Hands gripped the window ledge, bleeding over the shards of glass. Hazel scraped them off with the bar.

"It's got Gran's soul," Kelly said, tears rolling down her cheeks. "That's got to be how she was the first one. It changed her, and then all it had to do was let the corrupt keep creating more on their own."

"That's what it collects from them when they're in range," Hazel realized. "The souls they killed. And until it can get the souls, it feeds on the fear."

"It's always stronger after a body turns up on the lawn. The souls give it the most power." She fixed Hazel with an intense look. "Ghosts can't move on if they've got no soul, Hazel. I'll be done if it gets me. That's the end."

"You're asking me," Hazel said, pausing in her scraping efforts, "to sacrifice myself for you."

Kelly bit her lips and looked away, ashamed.

"Of course I will," Hazel said.

Kelly gasped and then buried her face in her hands as she burst into tears. Hazel moved to hug her, but failed. She threw the wooden spike in frustration.

"It's not even a choice," she assured Kelly, her voice stronger now. "No question."

The board over the attic collapsed and a zombie crashed to the floor in a heap. Kelly jumped. Hazel wrenched the dresser away from the door. The second zombie fell from the ceiling and bought Hazel time to kick the bits of dresser back out from under the crack.

The pounding stopped when her hand touched the doorknob, but her heart picked it up. With one last deep breath, she yanked it open and stepped out. The corrupt had stepped aside like greeters at a hotel, frozen in place. No reaching hands clawed at her from behind. At the end of the hall, the shadow hovered over the open floor, but it wasn't the shadow anymore.

Hazel looked into her own eyes, red veins standing out around the clouded blue like branches reaching for the sky. Her face was pallid and grinning, showing teeth stained red and bearing traces of human gristle. Thick globs streamed from her red hands. Her clothes, the very clothes she was wearing, were smeared and spattered with the same colour. Split open wide from thigh to shin, Hazel could see each layer of skin and bone under her left leg, like a corpse in a learning hospital. It looked like the leg would be her fatal wound.

She imagined seeing this nightmare as a child, and glanced over at Kelly. She was shaking from head to foot, but standing firm at Hazel's side. The shadow limped towards Hazel along the beam, dragging the destroyed leg. Hazel fought the urge to shove it off the beam into the basement. The screaming outside surrounded the house. Hazel pictured Morgan and Riva fighting back even as they were devoured. She could see Di striking out in the dark, helpless without her vision. She could see Jen trying her best, but failing to defend her. She saw the animals they had rescued cowering in the back of the shed, betrayed by the people they thought had saved them.

"The end," the shadow said, licking its lips.

It made a come-hither gesture and Hazel obeyed, stepping up to the last floorboard. It reached out a bloody hand to Hazel and stroked her face with the back. The blood was still warm, but Hazel didn't cringe away. She felt for the 'good hooks,' as Kelly called them, reaching out all around her to the people she loved. The blue cords pulsed with her grief.

The shadow opened its mouth and breathed her in. She saw spots in front of her eyes and heard the screaming inside its gullet. Her head lolled as black dots obscured her vision. She shut her eyes. When she opened them again, Hazel was looking at Kelly from the beam.

Her vision flashed, like when the shadow had appeared to move under a strobe light. She saw the corrupt seep into the house and drown Kelly in bodies, stripping her of her intestines as if she were still alive. The blood flicked onto the walls. Kelly was screaming, screaming at Hazel to stop. She felt a flame of fear leap to her throat, then remembered she could not feed the shadow.

"This is a vision," she said aloud, and her voice was three: male, female, and her own.

The corrupt heard her. They pushed each other to get to her. Hazel backed down the hallway, backwards along the beam. Corrupt shoved each other over the edge, falling into the black of the basement. Hands started to reach up, snatching at Hazel's feet, tugging at the flap of flesh on her torn leg. She cried out as a strip was ripped off and the snarling of the corrupt fighting over it came up from below.

Her back met the wall. More than one zombie was attempting to cross the beam to get to her. They were drooling with excitement. She couldn't reach the door to the master bedroom. Yet she felt the shadow weakening inside her. It was draining its power with the intensity of the attack.

"This is it," she said, and shut her eyes.

She shut her ears to the snarling and growling. She numbed

herself to the fingers pawing at her feet. She pictured her mom coming home from a night-shift with an exhausted face. She saw Kelly hugging Di in the school parking lot. She saw Riva flashing the middle finger at a group of teens who laughed at Hazel for being on the wrestling team. Then she saw Jen telling her how much she admired her, and felt her heart flutter.

Hazel imagined Morgan insisting that they carry the unconscious Hazel in the wheelbarrow, ever the bossy leader with her heart in the right place. She pictured the animals they had rescued, the dog so relieved at the sight of them. Then her fingers found Salt's collar on her wrist and she realized she might see him again. She saw Breanna letting go, and smiled. With one last breath, Hazel followed her own advice: she let go.

She lost track of the corrupt. Her muscles relaxed, letting her limbs drift as though she were floating on water. More delicious than anything else was the relief. It flooded her mind, washing anxiety from the corners. She didn't have to fight for her life anymore. It was over. She let go of her identity, forgot her own name, and accepted death.

Messages

Her cheek was touching something cold. She turned her head a little to the left and to the right, so that she felt the grit of dirt shift under her skin. Her head was heavy. She became aware of a hand touching the cold surface too, and when she moved it, she discovered that it was hers. She was still floating, but the cold was speaking to her, telling her this wasn't quite right. She opened her eyes and was suddenly Hazel again.

She recognized a dangling cord. There was a shelf behind it, a long wooden table that spanned the wall. She rolled onto her back and the whole world shifted with her, then steadied. There was an orange glow outside the window that flickered like spattering blood.

"Basement," Hazel mumbled, and looked up at the gaping hole in the ceiling above her, the beam a streak of black across her foggy vision.

Then she realized the rest of her body was not touching the cold. She was resting on something lumpy. She pushed herself up on an elbow which sank a little into the lumpy thing. Her heart roared back to life. She was lying across bodies.

She scrambled up, her ankles rolling and righting as they slipped off the bodies in search of the basement floor. The corrupt were sprawled in mounds under the hole. Hazel backed away, stumbling, until she reached a clear space. The bodies were still. She looked up to where lifeless arms were dangling over the edge and saw Kelly's frightened face.

"Hazel? Is it–is it you?"

"I think so." But as she said it, Hazel felt a weary sort of anger that was disconnected from her own emotions.

Kelly swung her legs over the ledge. "Are you alright?" she asked as she dropped to the floor with a grace that embraced her new identity as a ghost.

"Bit sore," Hazel answered, flexing her muscles. "Bit confused..."

"I think they're all dead," Kelly said, surveying the bodies with amazement. "When you fainted it was like they all turned off. Just—," she snapped her fingers, "—off."

Hazel stared at Kelly. "They didn't...rip you apart?"

Kelly raised her eyebrows. "Of course not. I'm already dead."

"Where is it now?" Hazel asked, throwing an uneasy look over her shoulder.

Kelly hesitated. "The last I saw it...you two sort of...breathed each other in... It was like you possessed each other."

Hazel felt the disconnected anger again, and realized what it was. "I trapped it." As the realization hit her, her heart fluttered with fear, and there was jubilation inside her. She toughened up and said to it, "I'll never feed you."

Kelly comprehension dawned on Kelly's face. "But how will you? You can't avoid fear, it happens every day."

Hazel shrugged. It was an effort through her exhaustion. "I'll just have to be brave."

There was a whooshing outside and water smacked against the window. Both girls jumped in alarm.

"What is that?"

As one, they climbed up the stairs to investigate. Hazel had to fight the basement door open because a few pieces of furniture were still piled against it. When at last she managed to squeeze through, they passed over more bodies on their way to the open back door. There, they both froze in shock. Prone, burning corpses filled the yard and the screaming that had seemed to surround the house made sense. Armour-clad police were now hosing down flames, rainbows glowing where the sun met water. The dog was gallivanting around the grass, enjoying the puddles. Near the shed was a group of paramedics. They were treating the girls.

Tears jumped to Hazel's eyes. The shadow's trick had worked; she had thought she was the only one left. It was only the terrible grief that had saved her from being scared. It was just as she had always thought: it was easy to die if you had enough to gain from moving on, and Hazel had thought she had everyone to gain.

"Riva," she croaked, and found her voice obstructed.

All four girls looked up and jumped to their feet. Di almost knocked over the paramedic who was shining a flashlight into her eyes. The blankets they had been wearing for shock fell to the ground. Jen broke into a run, leaping over flame and water to get to Hazel.

"Hey!" one of the police officers cried in warning, but the girls ignored her.

Jen buried Hazel in a hug that almost knocked her down onto the back steps. Riva, Di, and Morgan were next, piling on top. They touched her hair, patted her back, trying through touch to make sure she was real; that she was okay. Hazel laughed even though they were squeezing the breath out of her.

"I think I can see your shadow," Di said.

"What?" Hazel asked, pulling back in alarm.

"I can see your shape. I think my vision's coming back!"

Hazel sighed with relief and patted the cat, who had, of course, padded along beside Di. "I'm so glad."

A paramedic came and took Hazel by the arm, gentle, but firm. Hazel allowed herself to be led away for inspection. The girls gathered around and she told them what had happened, not caring that the paramedic could hear every word. The only thing that could make her blush was Jen's half-horrified, half-admiring gaze. It warmed Hazel more than the sun and the fire put together.

* * *

The community centre was on the south side of town. People had holed up there during the corrupt's attacks. It took two days for the girls to reach it by police car because they had to keep stopping to clear bodies from the road. The whole town itself was due to be released from quarantine soon, and divided families could finally reunite. Riva didn't have to wait that long. The second their police escort stopped at the blue building, Riva raced inside. Hazel followed, and felt a twinge of fear as she watched Riva's eyes dart across the crowd. Something inside her smiled. She fought it back down.

"There," she said, spotting Riva's mother by the open-mouthed shock on her face.

"Riva!" she shrieked. "Oh, my Riva! My Riva!"

People cleared the way. Their weary faces broke into smiles as Riva's twin brother and sister screamed at the sight of her and came tearing through the camp beds. The living girls, Hazel, Morgan, Di, and Jen, and the ghosts, Alexis, and Kelly, stayed off to the side. Hazel felt a pang that she would not be meeting her own mother that way. When she saw the hopeful expression on Alexis' face, she felt her spirits slipping further.

"She's not here," she whispered.

Alexis met her eyes with denial.

"Who's not here?" a woman holding a stack of papers asked. "Who can I help you find?"

Hazel gave her Alexis' aunt's name while Morgan and Di told another volunteer their own. Hazel found an empty bed to sit on while Di and Morgan waited, wringing their hands and craning their necks.

"So...she's gone?" Alexis asked, her eyes still on Hazel, and her voice hollow.

"I'm so sorry," Hazel whispered as Kelly sat down on the bed next to her.

"And Derrick?"

Hazel had forgotten about Alexis' brother. "That I don't know."

Alexis' sigh of relief was like a silent scream. "I have to find him!"

"Wait," Hazel said, but Alexis was already off. She turned to Kelly. "You should stick with her. This is going to be really hard on her, one way or another."

Kelly nodded and disappeared into the crowd. Hazel jiggled her leg, watching the tragedy of ghosts finding their family members and then being unable to hold them. It gave her a pit in her stomach. The nearest ghost was a middle aged man with his head in his hands. Her heart ached for him, and compelled her to sit by his side.

"Excuse me," she said, weaving around the beds, "can I help you?"

His head jerked up. "You can see me!"

Hazel gave him an encouraging smile.

"Please, you have to tell my wife—"

"Who is your wife?"

The man indicated a woman with a clipboard and a look of intense concentration. Hazel listened to the man's message, and then walked straight up to the woman. She didn't hesitate or worry about what the woman would think of her. Her gift had saved Hazel many times. It was time to use it to help others, not in secret, but out in the open, where she could do the most good.

"I'm Hazel Conners," she said, "and I can see ghosts. Your husband asked me to give you a message."

* * *

By the end of the week, Hazel wasn't sure if running from zombies or passing on ghost messages was more exhausting. Her reputation spread faster than the corruption had. In no time there wasn't a soul in town who didn't know that Hazel Conners could see ghosts. The community centre turned into one big séance in the evenings; families cried with their departed, or begged for Hazel's attention. She went to bed at night with a sore throat, a raspy voice, and a feeling of satisfaction.

One of the first pairs she reunited was Alexis and Derrick. On that first day, Kelly had had to fetch Hazel to help console Alexis. The moment she saw her brother, Alexis melted into a puddle of tears. He was sitting with a group of parent-less children, some entertaining each other, some grieving.

"Hazel, promise me," Alexis sobbed, trying to stroke Derrick's cheek as he sat cold as a statue on a bed, "Promise me you'll take care of him. He has no one now..."

"Of course I will," Hazel whispered, standing off to the side.

It was an easy promise when she herself had lost a sibling and a parent. A group home was opening for the orphaned kids. Hazel would be sent there herself until her birthday in a few weeks.

As soon as he was alone, Hazel spoke to Derrick. She approached him where he was reading outside, Alexis at her heels.

"Hi," she said, leaning against the wall beside him. "What are you reading?"

He showed her the cover, but didn't look up. It featured a teen boy and girl looking over their shoulders in a dark forest.

"Is it any good?"

He nodded.

"I'm Hazel," she said. "You're Alexis' brother."

He nodded again, but Hazel sensed a shift in his attention. She guessed he had heard of her.

"I lost my sister," she said. "And my mom. But I can still talk to my sister, and I...I have a message for you from Alexis."

Derrick fumbled his book, his eyes alive with hope, and Hazel wanted to kick herself for phrasing it that way.

"I have to give you the message because she died," she corrected. "She says she loves you, and she's so sorry she can't stay with you and be there for you. She wants to, more than anything. It hurts her so much."

Derrick had gone from alive to guarded in seconds. He reopened his book.

"Ask me something only she would know," she encouraged.

At first it seemed like he would ignore her. Then Derrick licked his lips and spoke what sounded like the first words he had said in days. "Where's Mom?"

Without hesitation Alexis replied, "Watching."

"'Watching,'" Hazel repeated.

For a moment Derrick looked shocked. Then his face crumpled and he buried it in his book.

"Hug him, for god's sake!" Alexis cried.

Hazel held him as tight as she could, so tight he couldn't break free if he wanted to. Her own tears squeezed through her eyelids. She held him tighter than she would ever get to hold Kelly again. In response, he collapsed against her and moaned into her shoulder until he had to stop for air.

"Look at me," Hazel said as his teeth chattered. His age and his pain were a heartbreaking combination. "Alexis and your aunt will always be your family. But you are my brother now, if you want me as another sister. I promised Alexis, and I'll promise you right now. I will look out for you. I will make sure you are always safe. Whatever you need. I promise."

His fist still clung to the back of her shirt, and he didn't let go for a long time.

Collected Souls

During the day, Hazel joined an excursion crew who went out rescuing more trapped pets, thanks to Di's advocacy. Her eyesight had not returned beyond seeing dark and light and the doctor said she was unlikely to get it back. Her mission was fueled by her need to be useful, but also by the love Rescue showed her. He slipped into the role of protector and guide dog with no training.

The latest rescue was a starving cat. It had survived on toilet water and whatever spare food had been left for it. Hazel observed Di as she tended to the animal outside its house. She was gentle and sympathetic, and seemed to have a second sense for the needs of the animal. Hazel was glad there was room for someone like her in a zombie-outbreak world. Di's father leaned over the tabby, joining his daughter. Like her new dog, he had refused to leave her side for days.

The Animal Rescue team was following the Clearance team. The Clearance team was taking down the barricades. During the attacks, Emergency Responders set up five layers of barricades, defending and abandoning where necessary. In the end, the barricades were successful in containing the outbreak to one city. The rest of the world was safe, and therefore in the dark about the true nature of the disaster. There was one last barrier to remove before the Animal Rescue team could save the rest of the city's animals. Then, when the remaining bodies of the corrupt were burned, everyone still alive would be permitted to go home.

"Hazel," Kelly said, appearing with a frown as Hazel watched Di and her father.

Hazel was leaning against the railing at the front of the cat's house. The rest of the crew were loading up the last of the day's animals into cages on the bed of a truck.

"Mmm?" she answered.

"How come you haven't seen Mom?"

"I've answered that a hundred times," Hazel replied, avoiding her eye.

"Mom wasn't ready to go," Kelly argued. "She wouldn't leave without saying goodbye."

Kelly wasn't the only one who argued this with Hazel. One woman had screamed at her until they both had been reduced to tears. It was not one of her favourite memories.

"She would if she thought it would be easier for us," Hazel said. "And she didn't know I could see ghosts. And we'd just lost Gran, Mom wouldn't have wanted—"

"Don't patronize me," Kelly said, facing Hazel with a withering stare. "The shadow...it ate her soul, didn't it?"

Hazel hesitated and that was all the answer Kelly needed. Her face crumpled. She wandered away, one hand over her open mouth. In miserable silence, Hazel watched her go. Some people weren't coming back because the shadow had collected their souls. Hazel could never admit it to their families. She hoped the souls were vindicated now that she was in control, but it still sickened her to think of all the people who were gone forever; the people devoured by the creature she herself had swallowed.

* * *

The quarantine was lifted. It was time to face homes with empty rooms. The return of internet and power meant the end of isolation from the rest of the world. The message went out about a virus that, while devastating, had been contained. Any mention of 'attacks' disappeared within minutes. The government didn't want unnecessary panic.

When Hazel's bus was due to leave the community centre for the group home, both of Riva's parents pulled Hazel into tight hugs.

"If you need anything," her mom said, "call right away."

"Let us know what you decide," her dad said.

They had made the offer to take Hazel in days ago. It was generous, but Hazel wanted to stay close to Derrick for now. Riva's parents waved away her gratitude, saying she had saved the whole town. Riva had shared everything with them, but Hazel was uncomfortable every time someone thanked her. She couldn't get used to the idea that so many people knew what she could do when only a few weeks ago her own mother hadn't known.

"Call me when you're ready," Morgan said as she embraced Hazel, and Hazel was surprised to see that her eyes were bright.

"I will," she said.

"And me," said Di.

"Okay," Hazel agreed. "We'll just get settled first."

"Okay."

No one seemed able to say more. Splitting up after surviving everything together was strange.

"I'll help you carry that," Jen offered, grabbing Hazel's bag of rations before she could protest.

Riva, Di, and Morgan hugged her one last time each, and then let her go. Hazel and Jen moved into the bus line. Derrick was waiting for Hazel there, which brought Jen up short.

Jen addressed Hazel as she shifted from foot to foot. "I just wanted to tell you that... Remember that night we were talking about who we liked? I mean I didn't at the time, but... I mean I was always..." She took a breath. "Whew, this is hard."

"What?" Hazel prompted, and the shadow swallowed her sudden fear like a drink to the dying.

"I-don't-like-boys," Jen said in a rush, her face turning a furious shade of red.

Hazel bit her lower lip to stop her smile, but the corners of her mouth betrayed her. She took her bag back from Jen, trying to be casual.

"So...talk later?" Jen asked, beaming.

"Definitely," Hazel agreed. If it weren't for the weight of her bag, she felt like she might float away.

Jen threw her another grin, and off she went. Hazel loosed the smile and it spread across her entire face. Derrick raised his eyebrows, teasing her with a look. She gave him a good-natured push towards the bus, and Derrick responded with a warmth that was coming back to him thanks to his dead sister.

Blue Cord

A few months later, Hazel and Derrick stood at the front door of Hazel's duplex. They had both moved in with Riva's family, and Derrick was back in school. She and Derrick had made arrangements for Hazel to pick him up from school so they could have a meeting in private with their dead siblings. Hazel took a big breath that shook on the way out. She struggled to untie the knot of dread in her stomach.

"This must be weird for you," Derrick said, shifting his backpack on his shoulder.

Hazel nodded. "I feel like when I open the door there's all this sadness that's going to come out and drown me, and I'm safer just staying out here."

Hazel realized by his silence that this was heavy for an already traumatized ten-year-old. Kelly and Alexis moved closer in support. Then, to her surprise, Derrick's hand slipped into hers. She passed him the key before she could chicken out and feed the shadow further.

"Would you...?"

"Sure," he said, sticking the key in the lock.

The door opened with a familiar squeak of the hinges. It was exactly as she had predicted. She was right back in the evening of Gran's death. Everything looked and smelled right, but it was too quiet.

Derrick led the way inside, taking in the stairs straight ahead and the kitchen to the right.

"Where should I put my stuff?"

"Here is fine, for now," Hazel said. Part of her didn't want him to touch anything. "I'll show you the living room."

She took him through the hall. On a side-table was the magazine Jolene hadn't finished reading, the remote stuffed inside as a bookmark. Hazel stalled, then passed the remote to Derrick. The moment it left her hand, the strange sense of loss turned to relief. It was one less ordinary object to place sad significance on.

Derrick settled in to watch cartoons with Alexis at his side. Hazel turned to Kelly.

"Ready?" she asked so the other two wouldn't hear.

Kelly grimaced, but trudged upstairs nonetheless. She wavered at the bedroom door and the sisters surveyed the mess. There were several glasses of unfinished water spread around the room, which Kelly was notorious for abandoning. The bed was unmade and a pile of laundry was seeping out of the basket in the corner.

"I can't touch any of my stuff, can I?" Kelly asked.

Hazel shook her head. Kelly pretended to run her hand across the surface of her dresser. She paused at her jewelry.

"I guess I have to give these to you now."

Hazel frowned. "Well, you don't have to."

"I don't mean it like that. It's just that I literally only wore that new necklace once. I sound stupid, but it's not just that... It's everything; it's unfair. It's supposed to be my stuff." She waved at the room at large. "Lots of this stuff was given to me. It's meaningful. I was supposed to enjoy it for the rest of my life."

"You don't have to enjoy cleaning up this mess either," Hazel joked.

"Well, you'll be paid well for it," Kelly said with more than a hint of bitterness.

Kelly sat on her bed, and looked even more disappointed that she couldn't feel the sheets. She ran her hands over her face as Hazel dithered over where to start.

"How 'bout garbage?" she asked. "What stuff do you not care about?"

It turned out to be a decent starting point. In no time they had a huge bag to throw out and had moved on to sorting more valuable items. Hazel kept pocketing or hiding little objects that Kelly didn't care for. She kept an old Barbie with its hair chopped off because it took her back to the days when they had played together. She even took a blue seashell Kelly had found on a school trip because she was so used to seeing it on Kelly's windowsill.

All at once, Hazel was crying more than she had since the attacks. She could feel that hole in her chest again, as wide and hideous as what they had done to the hallway in Jen's house.

"Hazel..." Kelly sighed.

"I'm fine," Hazel sobbed, getting up. "Just a minute."

She ran for the bathroom, but paused outside her mother's room. She couldn't turn her head and look through the open door.

When she recovered her composure, Hazel blew her nose and studied the dark circles under her eyes in the bathroom mirror. For a while after moving into the group home, Hazel had awoken most nights with nightmares. The shadow thrived on those moments when Hazel couldn't remember where she was, but she had gotten better since moving to Riva's. Last night she had had another restless sleep, thinking about today.

When Kelly's room was cleared, all four of them gathered in front of the master bedroom. Hazel took a deep breath, and they walked in together. This was the location Kelly had chosen, and Alexis agreed to. They sat in a circle on the floor, a ghost on either side of Hazel, and Derrick opposite.

"This part of dying," Hazel said, "doesn't hurt."

"Leaving all of you does," Kelly said, twisting her hands in her lap.

Hazel smiled sadly. "If you do see Mom and Gran, give them my love," she said. "If you have to think about us, think about how much it means to us that you can to do that. Think about Breanna. And your aunt, Alexis. Your mom."

"What if no one's on the other side?" Alexis asked.

"Then you won't be either. Nothing to worry about."

"And that's not a scary thought?" Kelly grumbled.

Hazel thought for a moment, then said, "No. Because there are no worries there either. It seems peaceful to me, to know that stuff will never hurt you again. It's either seeing the family members who've moved on, or it's complete peace."

The ghosts nodded nervously. They had already discussed this.

Hazel smiled. "Give Salt a kiss from me."

Kelly smiled too.

With all their squabbles, it was difficult to admit how much love was between the two sisters. As much as Hazel had learned about showing appreciation for the ones she loved while she had the chance, there were still walls to break down in her final moments with Kelly. She wanted to protect herself from the pain that went along with loving someone perhaps more than herself, and then losing them. Their old arguments were the only way to stay sane in the face of such love. But when the arguments were shed, the warmth and relief that came after everything had been said was worth the tears, the stuffy noses. It was worth the moment of beautiful, painful loss.

Then they all took a deep breath together, and began to meditate. Eventually, the blue cord that connected Hazel to Kelly faded away. Hazel could swear she could still feel it as she squeezed Derrick's hand.

* * *

At Riva's, Hazel embraced her new fame and was allowed to stick a sign into the front lawn, reading, 'Hazel Connors: Medium. Available 9–3 weekdays. Must have an appointment.' She scheduled five people per day, wanting to make sure everyone had at least an hour with their loved ones. It was her goal in each session to help both parties move on, but it was up to them how many sessions they would agree on before the final one. The customers understood that their payment was going towards Hazel's education as a grief counselor. Those whose loved ones never arrived, Hazel refused to see again. She couldn't take money from someone whose family had been consumed by the shadow, and she couldn't bear to explain the truth about why the lost loved ones weren't coming. She would give them a card for a certified grief counselor, and apologize as she saw them out the door.

Classes at the university were smaller than in previous years. They were also a more determined student body, and fierce supporters of each other. Jen was Hazel's greatest enthusiast.

They had one class together, where they sat beside each other and held hands under the table. The semester was coming to an end, and Hazel was going to miss the simple comfort more than she could say.

"Hi!" Jen said, setting down her bag beside Hazel the evening of their final, "are you ready for the exam?"

Hazel had been too busy with her medium job to study. Her stomach squirmed. She had an unexpected impulse to seize the plastic fork she was finishing her cafeteria pasta with and stick it in Jen's throat.

Jen gave her a knowing, concerned look and steadied her hand. She whispered, "Hey. Hazel Conners isn't afraid of anything."

She led Hazel through a few calming breaths.

"Thanks," Hazel sighed, feeling in control again.

Jen smiled and shook her head. "You can't get rid of me that easily."

Hazel rolled her eyes and groaned as they said together, "I'd come back to haunt you."

Their professor passed out the exam. Hazel pushed her empty plate away and the girls shared a quick kiss before getting out their pens. Hazel's heart flooded with calm, and the shadow sunk back down, far below the surface.

Read on for a sneak peek at book 2: Hazel's Mirror

Riley

Riley's bedroom was to the right of the kitchen, on the complete opposite side of the house from his mom's. He managed to stay in there all afternoon before she called from the kitchen that he would be in charge of his own dinner tonight. He snuck out now and then to get more ice for his bruised eye, and when it was dark enough, he joined his mom on the couch where she was watching TV with the lights off. Riley smiled when Charlie, his German Shephard, came and put his head on his lap.

They were halfway through an episode when Riley caught sight of someone in the dark kitchen doorway. He flinched so bad the couch springs squeaked and Charlie jerked awake.

"What is it?" his mom asked before the springs had even stopped bouncing.

She was so quick Riley hadn't gotten a good look himself. It turned out to be the familiar ghost of a little girl who sometimes passed through the house. She never spoke to Riley, just stopped to give a shy smile before running away again. He suspected she didn't speak English.

Riley let out a breath as he relaxed. "Just the little girl again."

His mother's face darkened as she settled back into the couch.

Out of the corner of his eye, Riley saw her jaw clench. He looked down at his hands, feeling, as he had so often before, like he had let her down.

After his dad's death, Elisabeth had attached herself to Riley's side for two weeks, waiting for Liam to show up. Each time she caught Riley flinching, her whole body had tensed with desperate anticipation. A tiny piece of Riley's heart broke every time he had to tell her it wasn't Liam; it wasn't Dad. He hated to see the pain in her eyes before she hid her face from him.

Over time, the pair had slipped back into their usual routine and then into the opposite: they spent almost no time together. The constant jumping, the continual let down; it was too much for either of them to bear.

In the light from the TV, Riley saw Elisabeth's hand tighten around the remote. She was grinding her teeth, and her breath was rapid, like she was winding up to say something. He chewed his lips, waiting.

At last, she paused the TV and twisted in her seat to look at him. Under the glare of her full attention, he froze in place, determined to keep his puffy eye out of sight.

"Has Dad visited you?" she demanded.

"No," he said in surprise. "I told you, it was the little girl."

"I meant ever," she snapped, waving the remote.

Riley shook his head, stroking Charlie's nose and avoiding her eyes.

"You're lying to me!" She sprang to her feet.

Charlie rose at the sudden movement and went to his bed in the corner, where he could have more peace.

"I'm not," Riley said, wounded.

"Yes, you are!" she shouted, her voice rising dangerously. Riley knew she was winding up to say whatever it was she had been holding in for months. "He wouldn't leave us when he knows what you can do! You've been keeping him from me! How could you do that to me? Look at me! How could you be such a selfish—"

She had crouched down in front of him to force him to meet her eye, and now she gasped. She could see his black eye. She mouthed wordlessly for a moment.

"How—?"

"I got in a fight," he mumbled.

"You got in a fight?"

"I didn't start it."

She grabbed his chin and turned his head this way and that, inspecting him in the dark before flicking on the light and trying again.

"I can't believe you," she hissed. "What were you thinking? When was this? Why didn't you tell me earlier? Why didn't the school call me?"

Her grip pressed a bruise, and he pulled away. "It was at lunch," he lied. "I didn't tell anyone."

Her eyes flashed. "And no one noticed this giant shiner?"

His cheeks flushed.

"You skipped class again!" she accused.

"I was having a really bad day," he tried to explain, but she cut him off.

"I am so sick of your behaviour!" She was upright and yelling again. "First you lie about your dad, then—"

"I didn't lie about Dad!"

"Then explain why he hasn't come to us!" She paced the living room. When she turned back to Riley, her eyes sparkled with tears. "Your father would never do this to me!"

Riley leapt to his feet, done with getting yelled at. "He's doing it to me too! It's not my fault he turned out to be an asshole!"

Charlie barked once, like an admonition. The colour drained from Elisabeth's face. For a moment she looked like she'd like to hit Riley.

Her voice trembling with suppressed emotion, she repeated, "He wouldn't leave us like this."

Riley was shaking with rage at both his parents now. He couldn't believe she was still accusing him when he had done nothing wrong. He had held his breath as much as she had. His hopes had been dashed time and time again, just like hers.

Riley was getting so worked up, a muscle was twitching in his chin. He couldn't express how deep her betrayal cut him. He gave her the dirtiest look he could muster, and stormed out of the living room.

"We are not done!" she yelled.

Riley ignored her and flew across the kitchen to the backdoor. He jammed his feet into his yard work shoes and threw the door open. It slammed against the side of the house. Elisabeth grabbed the sleeve of his t-shirt, but Riley wrenched away and sped off across the yard. Elisabeth didn't follow him, and he didn't look back.

The corn flashed past on one side, the chicken coop on the other, and before long Riley reached the woods. He stumbled on the pitch-dark trail. Without slowing down, Riley pulled out his phone and turned on the flashlight. The light zigzagged over the rocky, pine-strewn earth.

He hadn't planned it, but within half an hour Riley stood where his neighbours had found Liam's body. He knew it by the short brick well in the middle of the clearing. The well was green with moss and weeds, and only came up to his knees. It was a square hole just big enough for a bucket, of which there was none. The front bricks had collapsed into the well and disappeared into its dark interior. His light reflected off a metal sign in the dark. It stood to the side of the well and read, 'Caution, non-potable water. Do not drink.'

When Riley was a kid, this place had fascinated him. His dad told him there used to be a tiny house nearby, just a cabin, but the woods had long-since taken it back. Riley would come here sit beside the well waiting for ghosts and imagining how they must have gone about their lives. He had hoped to ask them questions about the old days.

The spirits were long gone; he never met a single one. Then, a week after Liam's death, Riley had come in search of a ghost again. Riley had thought, had hoped, that maybe his dad was stuck here. Now, as his flashlight roved over the clearing, the memory of disappointment bubbled like acid in Riley's chest.

Yet the next time he had visited here was worse. A month or so after their loss, Riley had watched Elisabeth disappear along the trail from where he was working in the yard. He had returned to raking. Some time later her anguished scream reached him through the trees. His heart had stopped beating in his chest, and he felt like all the blood in his body had drained into the dirt below his feet. Feeling close to passing out, he had forced himself to run the trail with the rake gripped tight in his hands.

By the time he arrived, both palms sweating on the handle, Elisabeth was sitting in the dirt with her back to him, hunched in front of the well. His eyes swept the forest for signs of an attacker, but she was alone. She moaned and rocked, both hands in her hair, and Riley stood frozen. Moms weren't supposed to make sounds like that.

The moan rose and morphed into a scream of rage. She

pounded the ground with her fists. In the next second she was on her feet, and faster than Riley could blink, had kicked in the front of the well. The bricks clattered and splashed on the way down. When she started throwing rocks in every direction, Riley had backed away.

Here he was again, and he could still hear the gong-like sound of one of her rocks pinging off the metal sign. The memory prickled; she was not the only one who had suffered. Riley wanted to rage like she had. He filled his lungs.

"DAAAD!"

If the woods had been quiet before, it was nothing to how they sounded after his echo faded away. Riley's heart ached as he flashed his light into the trees all around him, searching for his father. The light passed over the well. A dark face looked out at him.

Riley went cold. He refocused the light on the well, but the head-like shape was gone. He stared at the mossy bricks, his eyes making up faces in the surrounding leaves. Then, in the broken-toothed front of the well, long black fingers shifted. Riley's whole body tensed, the grip on his phone like a vice.

"R-Riley..." a voice rasped.

Riley's lungs were frozen. He drew in miniscule snatches of air as he watched the fingers. This didn't make sense. No spirits were ever here, and Liam's body had not been found inside the well.

His voice came out low and weak. "Who's there?"

"Riley..." the rasping voice called again, a little stronger this time.

The well's echo distorted the sound. Riley couldn't tell if it was male. Yet there was something familiar in it.

"Dad?" he whispered.

Plaintive and pained, the voice spoke again, "Why...did you... leave me?"

Riley gasped. He choked out, "I didn't! I didn't leave you!"

"Come...back..."

Wracked with guilt, Riley threw himself down before the well, wondering what hell his dad had been trapped in all this time. He looked down into the narrow, dark pit.

The head made of shadows tipped slowly to leer up at Riley. Its abnormally long and skeletal limbs were folded in a spider–like pose as it clung to the ledges. Riley knew a second of sheer horror before the shadow launched from the well, wrapping its sickening limbs around him.

About the Author

Nicole MacCarron was born and raised in the Fraser Valley of British Columbia, Canada. She has two degrees, in Education and English. When she is not reading, writing, or teaching her students how to read and write, she inevitably ends up in Ireland.

Interested in supporting this Indie author? Please leave a review on Amazon, or join Nicole MacCarron's mailing list to receive a <u>free short prequel to *Hazel's Shadow*</u>. To get your free short story and to find more books by Nicole MacCarron, go to the website listed below.

You can connect with me on:

🌐 https://nicolemaccarron.com
🐦 https://twitter.com/MaccarronNicole
f https://www.facebook.com/maccarronnicole
🔗 https://www.instagram.com/writersarereaders
🔗 https://www.tiktok.com/@nicolemaccarron

Also by Nicole MacCarron

Book 2 in the Hazel Series coming soon:
Hazel's Mirror

Hazel's Mirror

After last year's massacre, Hazel has spent a year suppressing fear and grief. So when the opportunity arises to get out of town and support her girlfriend in a basketball tournament, Hazel is quick to pack her bags. The weekend takes a dark turn when a mysterious boy begins haunting her and Hazel realizes they may have something sinister in common. As their worlds gradually intertwine, Hazel finds temptation among new supernatural abilities. Thrust into the unwanted role of mentor, she must test her new talent to discover if it will save them both, or destroy the last remaining people she loves and unleash her worst nightmare.

* 9 7 8 1 7 7 7 5 1 5 9 0 4 *